Because Stanley possesses a uniq ... ...ugination, he is marked as another victim for the satanic tyrant. While fleeing from this threat, our innocent discovers his soul while Alison, dabbling in the occult, nearly loses hers. The author has created a convincing world of magic, quantum and mind-blowing ideas in which to set an endlessly surprising adventure. Along the way, enormous questions are being asked about how power should be used, whether it is scientific or magical.
Gordon Strong, author of *Merlin: Master of Magic* and many other books.

The Last Observer is like *The Devil Rides Out* but on steroids. Magic and Science collide, dragging bookworm Stanley into a fast-paced adventure full of intriguing twists and turns and culminating in a battle over reality. Vasey combines ancient magic and quantum physics in a seamless picture of what reality might be and uses it as a theme to weave the devil of a story. It's a gripping and thought-provoking ride.
Alan Richardson, Author of *Magical Kabbalah* and many other books.

Gary tells a classic tale of mystery and suspense but weaves within it a series of themes that would be at home in any modern physics text book. He masterfully uses his own extensive knowledge of modern magical rituals to create a tale that is both mysterious and intriguing. However, the mystery soon gives way to something far more sinister and terrifying, a terror that explodes into a finale of epic proportions in which the fate of the universe itself is at stake.

Once started this book cannot be put down and once finished you may just find yourself checking the shadows to catch a glimpse of the Lord of the Elements.

Anthony Peake, author of *Is There Life After Death? The Extraordinary Science of What Happens When We Die* and many other books.

The Last Observer

Observer

A Magical Battle for Reality

The Last
Observer

A Magical Battle for Reality

Dr. G. Michael Vasey

Winchester, UK
Washington, USA

First published by Roundfire Books, 2013
Roundfire Books is an imprint of John Hunt Publishing Ltd., Laurel House, Station Approach,
Alresford, Hants, SO24 9JH, UK
office1@jhpbooks.net
www.johnhuntpublishing.com
www.roundfire-books.com

For distributor details and how to order please visit the 'Ordering' section on our website.

Text copyright: G. Michael Vasey 2013

ISBN: 978 1 78279 182 9

A CIP catalogue record for this book is available from the British Library.

Design: Stuart Davies

Printed and bound by CPI Group (UK) Ltd, Croydon, CR0 4YY

We operate a distinctive and ethical publishing philosophy in all
areas of our business, from our global network of authors to
production and worldwide distribution.

To the seekers of hidden knowledge everywhere, the way is long and hard.

Don't cut corners!

For Gabriela, Deni, Paul, Liam and Jon.

Foreword

by Anthony Peake

For centuries, there has been a secret, occult tradition that has developed in parallel with science. In their earliest forms both traditions were identical, a singular approach to reality that included both the outer, physical world and the inner world of thoughts and ideas. Indeed, for these early "natural philosophers" mind and matter were simply aspects of a deeper reality, and both were investigated using experimentation and observation.

However, whereas the physical objects that existed in three-dimensional space could be manipulated, broken apart and analyzed using systematic techniques, the inner world of thoughts and dreams could not be understood using this method.

Natural philosophy began to follow two separate paths. For a time a person could be part of both traditions, Isaac Newton for example. But as science began to define itself it found that only the physical world was willing to open up its secrets to those willing to interrogate it. Natural philosophy split into two seemingly conflicting world-views; the Physical and the Magical. The former developed into a process of understanding in which objects in the physical world were systematically broken down into their constituent parts (or elements). This technique, known as materialist-reductionism, has become the cornerstone of all the physical sciences. The only thing that exists are variations on matter and energy, and everything that is perceived is simply interactions between these two states. By understanding the relationships of the constituent elements, any physical system could be understood. In this materialist-reductionist world-view there was no place for anything that could not be measured or quantified.

The Magical world-view took a different approach. Its adherents believed that the world worked through the relationship of both objects and thought. Unlike Physical science, Magic proposed a model in which the physical universe was simply a manifestation of a deeper, non-physical reality and by controlling these deeper forces the material world could be controlled and manipulated. In other words, for the magicians thought was prime and physical reality was secondary.

From the time of Isaac Newton materialist-reductionism was in the ascendancy. Its process of understanding-by-breaking-down was startlingly successful. Not only did this technique explain much of the physical world but it also allowed scientists to create technologies by which that physical world could be harnessed for the greater good of all. From steam engines to medicine and from electricity to chemistry the power of materialist reductionism was self-evident. However, there were a handful of small issues that could not be explained by reductionism, issues that worried the scientists of the late 19th century. It was these small mysteries that were to bring about the greatest revolution in scientific knowledge. These mysteries were known as; Black-Body Radiation, the Photo-Electric Effect and the Emission Spectrum of Hydrogen. By 1905, Max Planck and Albert Einstein had explained these mysteries and, in doing so, had created a new model of science that reflected more closely the Magical than the Physical. This model became known as quantum mechanics.

Over one hundred years later the discoveries opened up by the pioneering work of Planck, Einstein, Bohr, Born and Heisenberg have created a universe in which consciousness and the "act of observation" seem central. We now know that "mind" is an integral, not periphery, part of how reality functions. Recent discoveries have suggested the existence of a "quantum vacuum", a place in which everything that is observed is encoded as information. There is also startling evidence that the universe is one huge hologram in which each part contains the whole. But the most staggering disclosure of modern science is that the universe needs an "observer" to continue to exist and that each "observer" may be responsible for their own sub-universe.

This is magic masquerading as science.

What is now needed is a novel that brings together our new understanding of science with the old beliefs of magic; a Dennis Wheatley novel for the 21st century. This is exactly what Dr. Gary Vasey achieves in this incredible book. Gary tells a classic tale of mystery and suspense but weaves within it a series of themes that would be at home in any modern physics text book. He masterfully uses his own extensive knowledge of modern magical rituals to create a tale that is both mysterious and intriguing. However, the mystery soon gives way to something far more sinister and terrifying, a terror that explodes into a finale of epic proportions in which the fate of the universe itself is at stake.

Once started this book cannot be put down and once finished you may just find yourself checking the shadows to catch a glimpse of the *Lord of the Elements*.

Anthony Peake

February 2013

Chapter 1

A Dead Psychic

There was something remarkable about Michael Kent. His crystal-clear and deep-set blue eyes, sunken into a pale and haggard face, seemed to penetrate into the depths of your very soul. He appeared to be capable of reaching inside of you so that he could search through your entire contents without first having had the courtesy to ask. Michael was a well-known psychic in those parts. Locally famed, and at the same time loathed, for his apparent ability to help the local constabulary solve unsolvable crimes. Yet now he was an unsolvable crime himself.

Kent had been found dead just outside of his favorite pub, the Rose and Crown. The back of his head caved in like a boiled egg, and the contents of his larger-than-normal skull splattered about the pavement. No one had seen how he had met this fate and the local police remained stumped. Even in death, those eyes glittered like opals as if taking in the entire world and reflecting it back out again. His untimely death made the front page of the local papers and had people whispering and gossiping for a few days. Who had killed Michael Kent and why?

Edward sat reading the account of Michael's death in an old copy of that paper in a dimly lit and rather damp room of the local library. Kent's face stared out from the page and Edward felt a strange sensation as if those eyes examined, and yes, even judged him. For Edward, this strange and unsolved crime was not an isolated incident but one of tens, or perhaps even hundreds of similar murders that he had stumbled on almost by accident. Psychics, it seemed, were dying in their droves and they were dying strangely.

Edward leaned back in his creaky wooden chair and, suddenly feeling as if his balance had been lost, he pushed himself forward abruptly, attracting the disapproving looks of his fellow library occupants. He went back over recent events trying to convince himself that there surely couldn't be anything to this wave of psychic killings. However, something deep inside told him there was.

Chapter 2

Imagination

Stan looked up for an instant from his book. The sound of torrential rain hitting the window had distracted his attention, and for a short while his eyes saw a streaky view out of his back window through the rivers of water running down it. He looked but he did not see, for inside his mind he was still watching the dreamlike images conjured up by the narrative that he was deeply engaged in reading. A sudden 'crack' of a window off its latch and catching the wind somewhere in the distance finally brought him out of his inner landscapes and imagination with a jump.

Stan put his book down. *Time for a cup of tea*, he thought as he made his way through his smallish and untidy flat to the kitchen. As he filled the kettle with water, his iPhone began to ring. He ignored it, hitting the button to kill the call while he popped a teabag in his cup and smothered it in boiling water. The phone began to ring once more.

"The bane of modern life," he said to himself, echoing a conservative politician in parliament. *Although that was no reason to try to slap a tax on the bloody things*. He recalled that the Government had indeed tried to tax mobile phones. He once again hit the button to kill the sound if not the call. He wanted to get back to his book. It was a good bit and he was enjoying it very much. However, the phone began to ring yet again.

This time he picked it up. The number shown was 'private'. Immediately, various thoughts went through his mind. On the one hand, he never answered calls unless he knew whom they were from, as he detested people hiding behind private numbers. But, on the other, it could be something serious, like a hospital or the tax man… He answered.

"Mr. Howard?" said a male voice. "Mr. Stanley Howard?"

"Yes – who is this?" he replied

Click! The phone went dead.

In annoyance, Stan threw the phone down and vowed never to answer an unknown-number call again. *I mean, the bloody cheek!*

The book Stan was reading took him in deep. He read in a trance-like state as images formed in his brain, conjured up by the author's words. He had traveled the world had Stan in his mind. Books were his escape from 'reality' into other worlds that he created and imagined into existence as the author talked words in his head. He had experienced everything more or less that could be experienced in life through his books but, more importantly, through his vivid imagination and inner picture building. He couldn't bear to watch movies as he found that they were simply a substitute for a poor imagination. For Stan, it wasn't just his ability to clearly see images because his imagination was able to factor in smells, sounds and all of the other senses. It was a veritable 4D IMAX experience for him, and this was why he simply spent almost all his free time with his head in a book.

Stan took a sip of his tea absentmindedly. He was struck by a thought that the tea, the physical tea he was drinking, didn't taste or smell half as good as the tea he could imagine. It was also the realization that, in fact, his inner world was more real than the outer that had turned him into a bookworm.

A book that he had recently read had surprised him greatly. It had suggested that the outer world, that he had grown to despise quite a bit, was also simply his inner world. He had read that, for example, images created in his brain resulted simply from light hitting his retina. The brain even managed to turn the image the right way up so that he didn't think he was upside down! This was apparently the way that light reflections from any object hit his brain – upside down. He was fascinated. It appeared that every image, every sound, every sensation was created in his brain and that his sensory experience was simply his brain's perception and interpretation of some cloud of atoms within a cloud of atoms. His mind struggled to understand this concept, but somehow he grasped it subconsciously. The real world, his world, was simply an image his brain constructed based on the signals it received. *Imagine that!* he had thought and then chuckled at his inadvertent joke.

At that point, the phone rang again. This time he had to search for the damn thing, which lay in a corner on the floor where he had thrown it amongst piles of books and unwashed clothes. Picking it up, he answered immediately.

"Mr. Howard?" said the same monotone voice.

"Yes", he replied rather abruptly.

"Be very careful, Mr. Howard." said the voice.

"What? Be careful of what?" But the caller had already hung up.

Stan was quite shaken. Who was this mysterious hidden caller and why the hell should he be careful? Why were such useless and slightly worrying calls disturbing him now?

Stan had had enough of his reading. His inner reveries had been shattered and he felt quite anxious. *A pint of bitter might help*, he thought, as he began to look for his coat and umbrella.

The pub was not very full but it was warm and dry. One or two people sat at tables chatting quietly in corners, while several others stood at the bar intently watching a football game on TV. He ordered his bitter deciding to stand by the bar.

"Hey, Stan," said a voice from behind him.

"Evening, Jimmy," said Stan, instantly recognizing the middle-aged but prematurely greying face of his neighbor Jimmy Bell. "How are you?"

Jimmy sidled up along the bar next to Stan. "Can't complain," he said in typical English fashion, which Stan took to mean that he would have to spend half-an-hour listening to a barrage of such complaints.

"What brings you in? No books to read?" asked Jimmy.

"Just needed to rest my eyes a bit, Jim," he replied.

"Can't be good for yer all that bloody reading," said Jimmy. "Missus is always complainin' 'bout her eyes when she reads those bloody women's books."

Stan smiled patiently and took a sip of his ale.

"Don't get it m'self," said Jimmy. "Dusty gloomy bloody things books if yer ask me."

Stan retreated inside of his mind as he vaguely listened to Jimmy's drone in the background still complaining about books, women, weather, and the England soccer team. Stan had no interest in any of Jimmy's ramblings and so he simply nodded or said 'yes' or 'no' from time to time. In his mind, Stan was imagining. He was imagining Jimmy having to go to the bathroom, imagining the peace and quiet that would ensue when Jimmy left. After a few minutes, Jimmy suddenly excused himself and ran off the men's room. Stan smiled to himself. *Always works*, he thought and moved to a vacant seat in a quiet corner of the pub.

Stan surveyed the scene, catching the three or four younger men leaning forward on their seats as they enjoyed a soccer game and a couple deep in conversation in the opposite corner. A few others were stood by the bar quietly sipping on their drinks, obviously lost in their own worlds of thought and imagination. However, Stan's eyes drew back over the bar to an anomaly. Something seemed out of place and rather strange, and he realized more or less immediately what it was. At the end of the bar stood a man dressed in a suit and tie.

How very odd, he thought.

He examined the man. He was tall and quite thin, almost gaunt. He had quite long black wavy hair that splashed over his collar and was swept back such that, periodically, he had to push the long locks back over his eyes into a more comfortable position. His suit was a dark blue pin stripe. He wore a white shirt, red tie, and polished black shoes. Furthermore, the man seemed to sense his incongruity because he seemed nervous and agitated, fidgeting with his keys while largely ignoring the beer on the bar. At that very moment, their eyes met across the room. For an instant, they locked stares, and then the man suddenly stood up and strode purposely across the bar towards Stan.

"Hi," said the tall stranger.

"Hello," replied Stan expectantly.

"Mind if I join you?"

Stan did mind, but he felt compelled to be generous and so found himself saying, "Why, of course you may."

The man went for his beer and keys that he had left on the bar, and swiftly returned to sit opposite Stan. He sat down rather heavily and immediately looked up into Stan's face. "Stanley?"

"Why, yes," said Stan, a bit shocked. "But how do you know my name?"

"Stanley, Stan? If I may?" the stranger said.

"Of course," replied Stan.

"Stan, I am so sorry to surprise you like this…" There was a pause as the stranger collected his thoughts. "I tried to call you earlier tonight but then thought better of it."

Stan was extremely puzzled and feeling increasingly uncomfortable.

"Stan, I have a lot to tell you and this may not be the place to do it," said the stranger, looking around and over his shoulder as if expecting something or someone.

"OK… And you are?" asked Stan.

"Oh good God, yes, I am awfully sorry, yes, I am Edward Bright."

"Pleased to meet you, Mr. Bright. You obviously already know my name," Stan said sarcastically.

Bright shifted his chair closer to the table and to Stan. Stan observed Edward's face and realized that Edward was again struggling for words. There was a strained silence as the two men peered at each other over their beers.

"What do you know about reality?" were the words that finally came out of Edwards's mouth.

"Sorry, what?" replied Stan in a rather bewildered and somewhat irritable manner.

"Reality," repeated Edward.

"Look, really…" Stan said, trying to comprehend how it was that a total stranger, a rather nervous stranger at that, could be introducing himself with such a bizarre question.

"Reality," repeated Edward, "what do you know about the nature of reality?"

"What's to know?" said Stan. "I mean, really. If you don't mind me asking, what on earth are you asking me? You call from a hidden number. You approach me in the pub. You know my name. Who the hell are you, and what the hell do you want?"

Edward looked glum and was silent for a while. Stan noticed that, in fact, Edward was older than he had first thought with deeply etched lines around his eyes, though his hair was not at all graying.

"The problem is, Stan, that I have something very important to tell you, but I am not at all sure where to begin," said Edward after some moments of contemplation.

"How about at the beginning?" quipped Stan.

Edward dropped back in his chair and stared into space for a moment. Then he cleared his throat and said, "Reality has to be observed by a consciousness in order to exist. Most 'consciousnesses' on our planet today are barely conscious of their own consciousness and therefore have a limited impact on the process of creating reality. Some, however – you included – are true observers." He stopped for a short while, eyeing Stan's reaction, and seeing no reaction began again. "There are some people, a group of people actually, who would like reality to be rather different than it is today. They are capable of making it different too – very capable."

Stan was hearing the words but he felt as if he was in a movie. It was an unreal moment. A total bloody stranger was telling him something totally bizarre. *This must be a dream*, he thought, but Edward was apparently on a roll.

"Imagine that a few people on this planet held the key to creating a particular type of reality – this reality – while another group desired a different reality. Plainly, there would be a conflict."

Stan held up his hand in complaint. "Wait a sodding minute," he said. "What on earth are you telling this to me for? It seems to me that what you actually need is a good shrink."

Edward looked shocked, again went quiet for a moment, and then simply said, "Stan, you are in danger. I need to try to explain why, and from whom, and I need to do it quite quickly. It is so important that our very existence, at least this existence, is under threat. I know that it sounds bizarre but trust me, I have been researching and following this for several years now and I am convinced that something very sinister is happening."

Edward's eyes and expression suggested to Stan that the man was genuine, but was that genuinely bonkers or genuinely concerned. Before Stan could contemplate this issue further, however, Edward asked, "Stan, would you come with me now? Let me show you something?"

For some unknown and very strange reason, Stan found himself saying yes. Stan was having a strong sense of *déjà vu*. Somehow, Edward seemed familiar; this completely bizarre, and perhaps silly moment, seemed very, very familiar. The hairs on the back of Stan's neck stood to attention and his heart beat loudly.

"Yes, I will," he heard himself say finally.

Chapter 3

The Evil Men Do

The room was pitch black and a heavy acrid smoke hung in the air. The voice droned periodically and there was a flash of light like lightning which, for a split second, lit up the altar and the hooded figure standing in front of it. The figure lit a candle and eerie shadows leapt up around the small room. An incense burner was producing acrid-smelling smoke and, as the figure waved his arms in a commanding motion, the smoke began to take on a form. A face seemed to appear, formed out of pure smoke. It was not at all human and it was only barely recognizable as a face with its two eyes, something that passed for a nose, and a wide leering mouth. The hooded figure lowered its head and went down on one knee. He pointed directly towards the face, but without looking at it, and droned another unintelligible phrase. The face stayed shimmering above the altar for just a few moments longer and then there was just smoke again.

For Zeltan, the words that had emanated from the face were clear, as if a quantum packet of information had just unwound itself inside his head. A smile crossed his face, still hidden underneath his hooded robes, as he understood the meaning of those words. He had a sense of satisfaction because he understood that the goal was near. Nothing could stand in their way now. Nothing. Just a few more eliminations and victory would be theirs.

His laughter filled up the room as he extinguished the candles. The room once again descended into pitch-blackness.

Chapter 4

Reality

In the back of the taxi, there was total silence. The London cab was past its best and the occupants could feel every bump in the road as it sped along through the rain. It smelled slightly of puke, vaguely disguised with the sickly sweet scent emanating from a card dispenser that hung from the mirror. Occasionally lit up by the headlights of an oncoming vehicle, Edward could see the pale face of Stanley Howard. Edward guessed his age at around 45 but he could not be sure. A few wrinkles around the eyes were the only visible clues as to his age since his hair was a dirty blond and, if he was graying, the gray hair was easily lost in the background color.

Stan did not look at all comfortable. Periodically, he would shovel his hair back while nervously licking his lips or pushing his small glasses back up his nose. Edward felt some sympathy for him, but he also felt compelled to ensure that Stan understood just what he and the world were confronting before the night was over.

It was already getting rather late and just a few people were out on the streets of washed-out London. Stan was plainly nervous as he followed their progress into town probably trying to guess their ultimate destination.

With a bit of a jolt, the black cab came to a halt outside a small hotel and while Edward busied himself paying the driver, he had half an eye on his reluctant companion. He was still worried that he may simply run off or change his mind. They both exited the cab and made a run for the doorway, but the rain was simply torrential, and the door would not open. They both got quite wet as Edward fiddled in his suit pockets for his key. Eventually, they entered the semi-darkened lobby of the hotel. Behind the counter, a young girl looked up from her book but lost interest as soon as the two wet men passed by the desk obviously *en route* to the elevator.

"OK?' asked Edward as he pushed the call button for the elevator.

"Guess so," replied Stan in a muted fashion.

Stan was quite tall and rather thin except for a bit of middle-age spread. Now, under the brighter lights of the elevator, Edward reappraised Stan's age as maybe somewhere in his late forties. Like many of the photographs that Edward was about to show him, Stan had very intense eyes. They were deeply set, and behind his glasses, their crystal blueness had a strangely compelling nature. They drew you in. The rest of Stan's face was rather nondescript except that he was very pale.

Not too surprising for someone who had spent most of his life with his head in a book, thought Edward.

Edward's room was just across the hallway from the elevator. Opening the door, he switched on the light and ushered Stan in. The room was typical of a mid-price London hotel. Very cramped and it had plainly seen better days. It smelled somewhat of a mixture of a hint of stale tobacco and very strong bleach.

'Sit, please make yourself comfortable," Edward said pointing to the only chair in the room. "Oh, but let me get you a towel so you can dry yourself a bit and maybe we should lose that coat too?"

Stan removed his wet coat and began vigorously rubbing the towel across his face and hair until, at some point, he felt drier. Handing the towel back to Edward, he sat down abruptly.

"Would you like a drink? I'm sure there is whiskey in here," said Edward as he bent down and started to open the small fridge-like mini bar beneath the wood-look plastic desk.

"Thanks, no," said Stan. "Look, it is really rather late, I'm now miles away from home, and I'm still not at all sure why I agreed to come here. You said that you have something to show me?"

Edward said "Yes," pulling about twenty or so colored card folders from a small bag by the bed and handing them to Stan. "These," he said.

Stan placed the folders on his knees and opened the top one. Inside there was a photograph attached to the inside cover of the folder, a newspaper cutting, and two pages of notes in very small handwriting. The photograph was of a mousy-haired woman, probably in her twenties, and the newspaper cutting had the heading *Mysterious disappearance of local housewife*.

He opened the second folder and found a similar arrangement, but this time the photo was a black-and-white grainy shot of an older man with gray hair and glasses and the clipping was in French. The third folder had similar contents.

"What is this?" asked Stan, finally looking up.

"Dead people," replied Edward. "Many dead and missing people."

Stan flushed and was obviously struggling to say something, which when he finally did was, "So what the hell has this to do with me?"

"I think you may be next," said Edward with a serious expression on his face.

Edward immediately understood Stan's reaction. Stan huddled himself in the chair, as if to defend himself, and looked as if he was about to jump and escape from the room. He plainly thought that he had fallen victim to a serial killer and conman.

"Whooaa, Stan, It's OK. I didn't kill them!" said Edward.

Stan looked hard at Edward and slipped deeper into his chair. "I'll have that whiskey now if you don't mind," he said, looking even paler than before.

Edward searched for glasses and finding them in the tiny bathroom, he poured two whiskies and handed one to Stan who knocked it back in one. Edward sat gently on the end of the bed and looked at his glass.

"Back home, I have an office full of similar files, Stan. Maybe five hundred or more," he finally said. "Each represents a person who has...*had* special talents. They were all very good observers." He shifted position, eyeing Stan to check his reaction. "All ages, all nationalities...all dead."

"But how? I mean, how do you know this? Why are you collecting files on dead people?" asked Stan.

Edward took a sip of his whiskey, savoring the heat of the distilled alcohol in his mouth before swallowing and then resuming his story. "It all started a few years ago, Stan, when two members of my Lodge were murdered. Oh yes, Stan, I am a magician. A real magician, but we can come back to that shortly. Other friends and colleagues died mysteriously or they simply disappeared over the next several months. They all shared certain, shall we say special gifts?"

Edward got up and reached for another miniature of whiskey, opened it, and poured the majority of the brown liquid into Stan's outstretched glass. Stan remained quiet watching Edward suspiciously.

"I started to get feelings, well shall we say more than feelings, sort of intuition that somehow these deaths and disappearances were related and so naturally, I started to do some research. The more I looked, the more I found out that extraordinary people had recently died, been killed, or had simply mysteriously vanished. I started these files on each of them searching for the similarities between them. That's how I came to certain conclusions...that there were certain similarities and characteristics between these people that led me to consider the unthinkable."

"What was that?" asked Stan.

"That someone wants to change our reality," said Edward.

There was silence and Edward played with his glass, spilling the contents from one side to the other as he allowed Stan time to take it all in and react.

Stan started to laugh. It started as a small giggle and then got louder and more like laughter. "Are you nuts?" said Stan. "You think someone wants to change our reality by killing people? Please!"

"That is exactly what is happening and if you will give me more time, I will explain how I arrived at such a hypothesis," Edward said, "and, more importantly, why I think you are next."

Stan's laughter abruptly stopped.

"Have you ever considered the nature of reality, Stan?"

"Not much," he lied.

"Reality is anything but real, Stan. It is just a dream."

Stan remained silent.

"Just a dream," repeated Edward, taking another sip of his whiskey. "Think about it. You are just a cloud of atoms inside a cloud of atoms. You are more empty space than anything else."

"Could be," Stan replied, "but I wake up every morning and I know I am me."

"Really? How do you know you wake up every morning, Stan? How do you really know that? Perhaps until the moment you awoke, you never existed but, on waking, you have memories that make you think you existed before yesterday."

Stan sat back in his chair apparently a bit more relaxed with a little alcohol inside his stomach. "I read a few books about that," he said. "I read one in which a man lived in this world, in this solar system and universe, and he came to know that he had a double, living on an electron flying around a nucleus inside an atom."

"Ah, the holographic universe!" said Edward.

"It was just a story in a book written by someone with a good imagination," replied Stan. "I also recently read that reality is inside of us, created by our brains."

Edward looked encouraged.

"Look, really, it is very late and I really have a long way to go back so, if you don't mind…" said Stan suddenly changing his mind about the situation. He wanted to leave.

"No," said Edward, "I have a lot to try to tell you and I am warning you, you are in danger."

"From whom?" asked Stan.

"I am not sure who but it can only be from a black Lodge," replied Edward.

"Black Lodge?" repeated Stan incredulously.

"Yes, a black Lodge, a group of black magicians."

"OK, now I know that you are completely off your rocker and I am wasting my time here... Black Lodge indeed?" said Stan indignantly. "This is the real world you know!"

"Real? Stan, that is what I'm trying to tell you. What is real? What is reality? What is magic other than the ability to change that reality through will?"

"Look, magic and all that stuff is great to read about in scary novels, and I have enjoyed a few Dennis Wheatley's myself, but that is all it is. I really, really cannot believe that I am sat here at," Stan pulled out his iPhone and glanced at it, "almost midnight on a foul night like tonight, sat with some paranoid stranger in his hotel room. What on earth was I thinking?" Stan stood up and put the glass down. "Edward, nice to meet you, old chap, but as they say please don't call me, I will call you," he said as he pulled on his still wet jacket.

"OK, Stan. We are getting nowhere I agree. But please, since you like to read a lot, take a few of these," he said, handing Stan several folders, "and read them, read some books about quantum physics, or the nature of reality, and please be very, very careful. Also, keep this and call me, anytime," he added, handing Stan a business card.

Stan took the card and pushed it into his coat pocket without looking at it. "Goodnight," he said, opening the door, stepping out, and closing it behind him. Edward listened to his footsteps across the hall, the elevator's arrival and then the elevator's doors closing, before sitting back down to think.

Chapter 5

Heat, Damned Heat

The Texas sun is hot. Hot as hell. In Houston, just a few miles as the crow flies from the Gulf of Mexico, it is also very humid. *Heat and humidity are a terrible combination*, Alison thought to herself as she walked from her air-conditioned apartment to her small BMW sports car. *Thank God for AC.*

The black leather seats were scorching and the leather-bound steering wheel even more so as she started the car. The air conditioning started up but it would struggle for a few minutes to counter the heat and humidity inside the vehicle.

Alison pulled out of her small driveway stopping briefly to push a CD into the player in front of her and then began to drive down the tree-lined suburban street in the direction of I-45. The volume was high and the bass notes were thunderous inside the small cabin of the sports car. Alison was feeling good. Her bags were packed and in the trunk of the car, and she was ready for the flight that lay ahead. As she drove, she cast her mind back a few months to recall the strange email that she had received.

"Hello Alison," it had said. "You don't know me but I certainly know of you."

At first, she had wondered if it was just a prank played by one of her friends but, as she read on, she realized that it could not be.

"Let me introduce myself," it read. "My name is Zeltan. I am a master and I have become aware of your magical abilities on the astral plane. I believe that now is the time to contact you and offer you some assistance and guidance."

The email went on to describe briefly the issues that Alison was facing in her mystical work and life in general. Whoever Zeltan was, the email stuck a chord with Alison. Besides, she believed in coincidences and in the fact that, when a student was ready, a master would present himself and so she had little difficulty accepting that the mysterious emailer was exactly what he said he was.

As she negotiated the car onto the I-45 south from the Woodlands towards Bush Intercontinental airport, she started to wonder what this Zeltan might be like. In his subsequent emails, it had become apparent that he truly was something of a master and that he certainly did seem to know a great deal about her life, interests and challenges. After several months of emailing and one or two amazing phone calls, she had been only too eager to accept the invitation to fly to London to meet with him.

During their correspondence, Alison had learned that Zeltan ran a small school consisting of several students from all around the world; each hand-selected and groomed by him. The school followed the hermetic tradition but the students, being so scattered around the globe, met only via weekly meditation sessions where each would follow the same meditational ritual. She had found this ritual particularly powerful and had glimpsed in her mind's eye a number of her fellow students faces as well as that of Zeltan himself, whose contact was extremely strong. At times, she had sensed his presence even during normal waking consciousness and had even thought that perhaps she had heard him speak to her from 6,000 miles away. She had already learned a great deal from Zeltan and his so-called School of the Elements.

As Alison checked in for the flight she was feeling extremely excited, and had to remind herself that such feelings should be kept under control at all times, but despite her best will she could not suppress the almost pure ecstasy flowing through her veins. Not only was she finally going to meet Zeltan, but she was to be initiated by him personally.

Alison found herself a seat in the waiting area and checked her watch. There was still quite some time to wait.

Growing up, Alison had been different to others. As her school friends started dating, partying and drinking, Alison had spent her time reading books on the occult and other esoteric topics. When she was not reading, she was meditating and recording as much as she could in her magical diary. Now she was 32 and she was still single. She barely had any interest at all in the normal life that most people her age lived. Instead, she had developed certain philosophies about the world and her purpose in being there, so she had little time for the materialistic pursuits of her old friends. Despite that, she had managed to get through college and had a reasonably paid job as a PA to a partner in a large consulting firm. It allowed her to rent a small apartment in the affluent suburbs of Houston. It had funded her one and only materialistic weakness; the small sports car that she owned. For her, driving was almost meditating and much better when driving fast!

Alison had come to understand that everything was really one thing. Everything and everyone was connected. She sometimes experienced this oneness in her daily meditation work. She had learned how to travel in her mind; visiting people and places in this world and others, learning about herself and about the world in the process. She had also understood how to listen to her inner self and ignore the attractive pull of the outer world. She felt at peace, but she wanted desperately to learn what she called real magic.

As a sole practioner, without any friends with similar interests, without membership of a group, and without the ability to do group ritual work, Alison felt she was missing something. Real magic was not just about 'knowing oneself' and becoming who you truly are, but also the ability to effect physical changes at will. Something she had read about but never witnessed nor succeeded in doing herself. Something Zeltan had promised he could teach her, she recalled, feeling that rising surge of excitement again. She had come to understand that there were two types of magic: mystical magic whereby magicians could change themselves via the will; and physical magic in that a magician could cause an effect in the environment beyond them. She felt that she had done much to master the former, but had made no progress whatsoever with the latter. But soon, very soon, she hoped that she would.

As the Boeing 777 moved off down towards the runway, Alison took one last look outside. The blue sky and the green lushness of the grass around the airport could deceive one as to the terrible hot humidity of Houston, she thought. The engines roared as the plane began to accelerate down the tarmac into flight and Alison smiled. In a just a few hours, she would meet the man who could change her world.

Chapter 6

Morning Discovery

Stan woke up abruptly. He struggled for a few moments to dispel the total fear that had come with him into wakefulness from the dream he had just experienced. He had dreamt of what he could only describe as hell on earth and he, Stan, had helped to create it. He could no longer recall how or why, but he still felt the remorse and sheer guilt because of it. However, as he began to wake up, he found he had another issue. There was a little man inside his head with a hammer and he was beating the crap out of the inside of Stan's skull. *That bloody whiskey*! He couldn't drink whiskey and this was the result – a nasty hangover.

Stan lay back in bed and closed his eyes. This was going to be a bad morning, he thought to himself. He rubbed his head and tried to massage the pain away, but to no avail. He stumbled up and out of bed and staggered down the hallway to the bathroom to relieve himself. He knew that he had some headache pills somewhere in the cupboard but he would have to find them. Then he had another idea. He turned himself around and sat heavily on the toilet seat. Lying back against the wall, he closed his eyes and started to imagine he had no headache, no pain. He sat like that for several minutes – willing, feeling, and imagining no pain, no headache. He simply decided with absolute certainty that he no longer had a headache and then abruptly stood up and marched off to the kitchen to make some tea. By the time he had made the tea, he was already beginning to feel much better.

For a moment or two, Stan watched the steam rising from his cup. He was thinking about the evening before. That strange meeting with the man called Edward in the pub. The strong feeling of *déjà vu* that had – eventually – compelled him to take a trip into town with a complete stranger, only to discover the man was obviously suffering from some sort of a mental disorder. He had delivered the news that, somehow, his life was in danger. *Utter nonsense,* Stan had thought. Now, in the cold light of day, he couldn't help wondering if Edward did know something. *After all, he did know my name and I never did get to the bottom of that issue.* He sipped his tea. He liked tea but once again realized that he preferred the imaginary tea that he dreamed up in his mind. It tasted…well more like tea. Stan decided to take a closer look at one of those files Edward had given him but then decided that after breakfast might be better. After all, he was suddenly really very hungry.

The photograph was of a middle-aged woman. Nothing extraordinary except maybe the eyes. The eyes were compelling. *They draw you in somehow,* thought Stan, chewing on the last of his boiled egg. There was a news clipping. Several in fact, as the woman turned out to be a celebrity who had been found battered to death in an alley around the corner from her London flat. There were no suspects and no apparent motive. Stan's attention then crossed to a page of handwritten notes. The writing was extremely small and written in pencil. The notes were difficult to read and Stan had to get his reading glasses in order to read them.

Member of the School of the Elements – a black Lodge headed by someone by the name of Zeltan read the first line. The name Zeltan was underlined and another note by the side of this read, *Seen that name before… But where?* Underneath that was written *20+ years practice as a magician and author of two quite well-known books on magic and reality. Reputed to have several gifts including being able to set fire to objects by force of will… Accomplished then! Associate of William Haps and Bridget Rice (both also dead – murdered in 2009). Observer? Certainly seems so.*

There was nothing more. Stan stood up, taking the file over to his rather old PC and called up Google.com on his browser. He looked again at the file cover. It read *Sandra Bellger.* He entered her name and searched to find about fifty pages, all relating to two books available on a variety of book-selling sites. *Mackical Reality* was the name of one while the other was entitled *Elemental Magic*. He soon learned that, in fact, this was a pen name and that her real name was Cynthia Collins; an actress in a TV soap opera that had ceased production several years ago. *Poor Cynthia*, he thought to himself sitting back in his chair.

He picked up another of the files. Again, there was a photograph, this time of an old man. Again, the man's eyes had a certain quality as if looking through rather than at you. He appeared well into his seventies and, in the photo, he looked happy enough. There were several small clippings including an obituary from a local paper.

Joseph Millington was a local business leader of some esteem, it read. *He was well known not just for having ran and managed Millington & Smythe, a local law firm, but also for his contributions to the local community in the form of his charitable work for several children's homes in the area. Mr. Millington was also an accomplished artist and had enjoyed some success with his oil paintings that focused on mythology – another strong interest of Mr. Millington who, in his spare time, lectured at the local community college on myth and reality. Mr. Millington leaves a wife and two children.*

Millington, it seemed, had also died suspiciously after a car in the street hit him outside his home in Beverley, East Yorkshire. It was a hit and run and the driver was still at large according to a clipping from the Hull Daily Mail. Stan flipped over to the handwritten notes. *Strong interest in mythology and its meaning for modern cultures – lectured on the topic and reputed to have a large library of rare texts and books on the topic. No connection to any occult organization as far as I can tell but given his interest in mythology… Linked, however, to Martha Hemingway who certainly had supposed psychic abilities and demonstrated mediumistic qualities. M. Hemingway was a close friend of Millington's wife and they must have met as a result. Eyes are interesting… Possible observer?*

Stan took another sip of his now lukewarm tea and sucked it back and forth between his teeth, a habit he had acquired when thinking deeply. *Observer*. The files repeated that word many, many, times and Edward had used the term as well, so what exactly did it mean?

Is there really any linkage between these two people other than in Edward's imagination? he asked himself.

He quickly scanned the third and final file that Edward had insisted he take. He found the same word again with a question mark in the same small handwritten scrawl. Accompanying the notes were a photo and press clippings for one Antonio Salzio, who appeared to have lived in Italy. This made the clippings rather useless, as Stan could not read any Italian. He shifted position in his seat and typed *observer* into his browser, but it brought up a bunch of newspaper sites and nothing of immediate relevance or interest. He sighed and then had another idea. He entered the words *nature of reality* and that query brought up a lot of very interesting and very bizarre websites and articles.

After about an hour of reading, Stan sensed something that he recognized as excitement.

With all the reading he had done in his lifetime, how the fuck had he missed this topic? he thought, as he got up to boil another kettle.

OK, real tea didn't taste as good as his imaginary tea but it was wet and warm and sipping on it, sucking it through his teeth, helped him concentrate – and concentrate he felt he must. As the kettle warmed up and he sought out a tea bag for his cracked and old mug, he was recalling what Edward had asked him to read about – quantum physics. For Stan, much of what he had just read made little or no sense but something had struck a chord. He had discovered that all was not as it appeared. Apparently, particles such as atoms, photons, and so on could behave as both waves and particles. The interesting thing was that the form they took seemed to have some direct relationship to whether or not a consciousness actually OBSERVED them. There was that blasted word again…

Stan had read of an experiment in which photons were fired at a barrier with two slits in it. In order for the photons to pass through the barrier, they had to go through one or other of the slits. As these photons were fired at the barrier, the natural conclusion was that two spots of light would appear on the photographic plate on the other side of the barrier, matching exactly the position of the two slots. In fact, what was actually observed was an interference pattern and not two spots. According to the explanation he had read, although the photon was fired as a particle and arrived as a particle, somewhere between setting off and arriving, it rather behaved as a wave passing through both holes in order to create an interference pattern. Light, it seemed, exhibited a duality of both particle and wave. Apparently, other particles behaved similarly; including atoms. Even more mindboggling was the follow-up experiment in which detectors had been placed at each slit to see how this could be. However, when the detectors were present, the interference pattern disappeared altogether and just two spots were observed as if the photons had acted as particles the entire time. If the detectors were removed then, hey presto, there was the interference pattern. If in place, just two spots. The conclusion drawn from this had simply blown Stan away. Unobserved photons behaved as waves but observed photons behaved as particles. One article had used the sentence that the very act of observation by a consciousness somehow 'collapsed the waveform into particles.'

Stan poured his tea and glanced out of the window. An amazing azure sky and bright sunshine had now replaced the rain and wind. The world looked clean and new to his eyes. His observation of external reality was, however, pulled back inside his skull as his thought processes took off once again. He had also read that particle pairs were somehow connected. Even more bizarre was the fact that apparently, when one of the two particles was observed, it seemed to dictate the behavior of the other. To Stan, the idea of observing had taken on a new level of importance and having made his tea, he returned to the PC and began typing new search terms somewhat feverishly. He read avidly about things such as Schrodinger's cat in the box and about quantum entanglement. He discovered that there could be an infinite number of alternative realities. There were so many other findings and hypotheses that it just boggled his mind.

By the time Stan looked up again, his tea was stone cold and his stomach was telling him that it urgently required filling. A quick look at his phone showed it was already 1pm. Stan scratched his head, marveling at how fast time went when occupied. His mind was flying and full of different bits of information that didn't yet all add up, but that had left him somewhat shaken. Nothing was as it appeared, and the more he had read the more questions had come to him during his research. Perhaps now was a good time to take a break and try to synthesize what he had learned.

With his mind so pre-occupied, he wasn't feeling inclined to prepare anything elaborate and so he cut himself two thick slices of bread and smothered them in butter and some cold ham from the fridge. He sat at his kitchen table and tucked in heartily.

What had he learned? Well, first, he already knew that his reality was created and existed inside his brain. Everything he saw, touched and smelled was conjured up by his brain. His reality was not 'out there' but rather inside his head it would seem, according to the book he had recently read. He also knew that reality, whatever that was, was simply a cloud of atoms and molecules including his own body and for that matter, his own brain. Somehow, he was sensing his environment and interpreting it into images and sensations that he could name; be it a color, or a smell, but whether any of it was really real was anybody's guess. There were even suggestions on the internet that he was living in a holographic matrix of multiple realities existing side by side in multiple dimensions. His brain hurt from even trying to put all of his thoughts together. The sandwich was gone and just a few crumbs remained. He absentmindedly licked a finger, stabbed each of the crumbs and put them in his mouth. He was still hungry but he had no will to prepare more food. He wanted simply to think.

It now appeared to Stan that Edward's claim that reality had to have an observer had some basis in factual science.

If a tree falls in a forest and no one is there to observe it, does it make a noise? he thought, echoing something he had read.

Stan wondered in fact whether, without someone to observe the forest and the tree, they actually existed at all in that moment. The more he thought the more confused he became. At the same time, he was convinced that *his* reality had just changed because of the morning's research. Quantum physics seemed to suggest that an observer was necessary in order for a solid reality to exist, but Stan had also learned that that observed reality actually only existed inside his mind. Further, there was evidence that his brain probably 'dumbed down' this observation of reality so that he could sense it in a way that didn't overwhelm him. There was also a suggestion that Stan's present moment was, in fact, already the recent past, as it appeared that the brain took some time to process this information, select what it deemed relevant, and present that to his consciousness.

We create our own reality, he finally concluded.

The idea that an observer created reality raised many other questions in Stan's mind. How, for example, did he share this reality with others then? Were the others the he shared reality with actually real? What did Edward mean by the term 'observer'? Surely, everyone observed and created their reality? The questions came quickly, one after the other until Stan groaned in the agony of chasing impossible thoughts to an impossible set of conclusions. He sighed deeply as he finally reached for the business card that Edward had given him the night before. There was no real choice. The only person who could answer some of his questions was the man who had forced him to ask these questions in the first place, and that was Edward. As he tapped Edward's number on his phone and waited for the ringing tones, he remembered that tomorrow was Monday and he would have to go to work, so any question-and-answer session would need to wait until at least the following evening.

"Stan?" said Edward's voice. "I've been expecting your call."

Stan wasn't surprised.

Chapter 7

Arrivals

Alison was very disappointed to find that Zeltan was not, as promised, waiting to pick her up in the arrivals area of Heathrow. Instead there was a driver holding a sign with her name on it. She made her way over to the man and then followed him through the crowds of newly arrived passengers and waiting greeters with a feeling of importance. A chauffeur was picking her up at least.

The drive seemed extremely long. She was tired as she had not managed much sleep on the plane, and instead had spent most of a shortened night reading a book. The limo was warm and she could feel her eyes beginning to close as tiredness began to overwhelm her. She was, however, determined not to sleep, so she switched position and rolled down the window to let in some air. London was busy but then again it was Monday morning, she thought as she absentmindedly looked out of the window.

Alison smiled to herself as she watched the city of London running around. *So many ants*, she thought to herself, *sleepers*. There was disdain in her imagined voice as she mentally said that word. Sleepers were people glued totally into a physical and material world. They were people who wasted their precious lives chasing wealth, flesh, power and influence never for a moment questioning why they existed or more importantly, how they existed. For all of their acquired wealth or power they were still poor and they had no real power. They were on the treadmill. There, they pedaled like crazy singing their master's song. They did not know that they had a master, or that they could hold his tune, but the truth was that they were automated morons giving power to their betters and masters.

Poor brainwashed bastards, she thought to herself with a sense of pity. Chasing the material when they couldn't take it with them and not actually seeing the real treasure that lay before them. *What was it that Jesus had said?* she pondered. *Something about not throwing pearls before swine.* As she watched from the window of the limo, all she could see were swine – hundreds and thousands of them.

"Here we are, madam," said a voice that jolted her from her thoughts. She turned to the driver and watched as he got out and opened her door for her. "Your hotel, madam." Alison was relieved. She would shower and take a short nap, she thought to herself as she took the bag that was handed to her from the trunk of the limo. Suddenly she really felt exhausted.

When Alison reached her room, she simply wanted to sleep. The large bed looked inviting and the en suite bathroom was well equipped with both a bath and shower. The question was which to use? Before she had had a chance to decide, the phone rang.

"Hello?" she said.

"Hello, Alison, and welcome to London," said the almost hypnotic and smooth voice of Zeltan. "How are you feeling after your trip? Tired I suppose?"

"Hello," Alison gushed. "No, I'm fine," she lied in the hope of speeding up a meeting.

"Alison, I have been detained by some unfinished business and I'm afraid we can't meet until the evening as a result. I will stop by your hotel at 9pm and pick you up for a late dinner."

Alison felt waves of disappointment washing over her as she heard those words followed by the click as Zeltan hung up. *OK. Well then, a bath.*

Chapter 8

A Revelation

Stan watched absentmindedly from the window of the coffee shop that he had agreed to meet Edward in, as people bustled by. The latte that he had ordered was too hot to drink and so he warmed his hands on the large mug while he waited. He had so many questions but where to begin? From his vantage point in the window, he saw the tall and rather gaunt figure of Edward arriving. He was again wearing a suit and tie under a Crombie-type coat. He looked quite suave and sophisticated, Stan thought. Edward saw him through the window, raised a hand to his head in a quick salute, and smiled broadly. Plainly, Edward was happy to see him.

Edward sat down opposite Stan after carefully removing his coat and placing it on the hanger thoughtfully provided in the corner of the coffee shop. He carefully arranged his suit jacket as he sat in a way that would minimize any creases and checked his watch. "Sorry, I am a few minutes late," he said smiling. "The tube was absolutely packed." In fact, Stan wasn't aware that Edward was late at all, as he had been deep in thought.

"No problem."

Edward looked into Stan's face. There was expectancy about the look. "I am sure that you have many questions, Stan, but take your time. I have as long as we need."

Somehow, Stan did not like this feeling that he had around Edward sometimes. It was a feeling that Edward was entirely in control and knew exactly how Stan felt.

"Well," he began. "I have been doing some research along the lines that you had suggested." He paused to think. "And, I have reviewed the files that you left with me as well." Stan could feel Edward's gaze. "What do you mean by the term observer?" he asked.

"Well, an observer is someone who has the power to create reality," replied Edward.

"But, everyone creates their own reality so everyone is an observer surely?" said Stan impatiently.

"That is true to a certain degree but some people really do create their reality. By that, I mean that they have a special talent for it. Their imaginative faculties and their magical skills are developed to the point that they really influence the co-reality that we all live in." Edward leaned back in his chair and took a sip of the coffee that he had ordered on his way in. "Some people have deliberately honed these skills often through years and years of practice while some are simply born with a latent gift."

"Magical skills?" Stan asked somewhat indignantly. "Magic like in Harry Potter?"

"Yes, I had detected your cynicism," said Edward dryly. Edward shifted in his seat as if to find a more comfortable position and rubbed his chin with his hand, his eyes staring into space as if struggling to find the right combination of words. "Magic is said by some to be the art of causing changes through the application of will," he said after a short while. "For me, I think there are actually two forms of magic. The first is where the practioner attempts to change himself and in doing so changes the way that they perceive their reality. You probably now understand that by changing your perception of reality you are, in fact, actually changing reality?" Edward didn't stop for an answer to his rhetorical question but rather proceeded to explain, "The other form of magic is physical magic in which the magician actually attempts to willfully co-create reality."

Stan listened carefully while studying Edward's expression looking for any hint that he might be pulling his leg, but all he saw was Edward's sincerity. He thought for a moment. He could, he supposed, give some credence to the first type of magic as it was in a sense akin to self-psychology and positive thinking and he had read quite a few books in that vein. But physical magic, now that was Harry Potteresque wasn't it?

"The first thing a good magician needs to do, amongst other skills, is to know himself. To dissect himself bit by bit, the good, the bad and the ugly. He has to know who he is and why he is. This is achieved through various forms of meditation and reflection, which, by the way, is another skill the magician needs to learn. By understanding himself, he can begin the Great Work of turning the inner lead into inner gold. In doing so, he is liable to discover that nothing – absolutely nothing – is what it seems to be. It can be both a mentally and emotionally challenging experience to go through this process, believe you me," said Edward. "As the process, which can take years, decades, entire lifetimes, is followed through with discipline, the magician will come to understand many truths and these truths come from within. He must learn them himself and can only be gently guided and taught certain techniques for it must be the magician himself that makes these realizations."

Stan was by now fascinated as much by Edward's sudden utter sincerity and demeanor as he was by the content.

"If the student is lucky, he or she will discover the inner voice. I say voice, but quite often the inner self communicates not with words but with pictures – images. Unless you have actually experienced it, it is very difficult to describe and it is one reason why old alchemical texts are indecipherable and use a lot of pictures or images and symbols. Only someone who has had similar experiences and realizations can actually grasp the meanings written in these old texts." Edward went on, "It's where our business gets its reputation for silence and secrecy I think. It isn't called occult without good reason as that word simply means hidden. Now the vast majority of humanity never glimpses this inner occult world. Instead they live as if in a dream, sort of living on automatic pilot guided by base emotions such as fear, greed, and anger and so on."

Stan interrupted. "So you are saying that the vast majority of people don't really create reality but simply sustain it through their emotional reactions to it then?"

Edward paused and considered the statement a while. "Yes, sort of," he replied finally.

There was a period of silence as both men contemplated the discussion and considered what still needed talking about. Stan surveyed the coffee shop with its clients happily engaged in conversation over coffee, or the odd customer engaged in a lonely conversation with their phone or tablet. Suddenly, they did seem to him to be oblivious, completely oblivious to the world around them. Each was in their own little world filled with important things and activities yet missing the obvious. The world controlled them rather than the other way around. But Stan was just the same as them surely? For him, books were the important things that filled his life and gave him a reason to exist. If not for books, what would he have? Nothing. He was alone. No real friends, he had never married, he had a dead-end monotonous job. He too was stuck in the dreamlike quality of day-to-day life.

"But these people are important too," Stan finally commented trying to justify his own self as much as anything.

"Of course they are. All of these people have the potential to co-create their reality if they really want to. They just have to ask some basic questions of themselves and wake up from their dream world. Eventually, some of them will and the rest will have many future opportunities to wake up. If not in this incarnation then certainly in the next," replied Edward.

Edward paused a while knowing the thoughts that Stan was experiencing. After a while, he began again. "Know thyself is the age-old instruction. In knowing yourself comes the connection with that inner self who is without ego and is a part of the All. The perfected self."

Stan remained silent waiting for Edward to continue.

"All is one and reality is consciousness experiencing itself," Edward said. "Of course, one can learn these techniques and chose to turn one's back on the connectedness, or oneness, and try to continue to serve self and perhaps this is the difference between white and black magic." Again, Edward paused for a moment, catching a twitch of an expression on Stan's face that betrayed a lingering sense of disbelief. "Now, imagine that you changed yourself and became one with the will of the All, with the will of the One Thing. What sort of reality would you be creating?" asked Edward.

Stan was thinking exactly that thought or at least trying but quite honestly, he couldn't fathom it. He could imagine having God-like qualities and then annihilating the first bastard to cut him off in traffic, which probably wasn't exactly what Edward had in mind. Stan reminded himself somewhat painfully that he really didn't much like people and certainly preferred the company of his books.

"How do you know all of this?" was what Stan finally managed to say.

"I am a magician, Stan. I have worked on knowing myself and on understanding the forces at work in the world and, I have some level of command over them. I found you on the Akasha."

"The what?" replied Stan.

"Akasha," Edward repeated. "It's like a record of everything and everyone that can be accessed if you know how to do it. A recording of everything in reality – of everything in *every* reality. That's where I learned of you and your remarkable abilities, and also of the danger that you are in."

"Remarkable abilities?"

"Yes. You have a tremendous imaginative faculty as well as a natural ability to create your own reality. Your inborn ability to observe and then co-create. Imagination is the key to magic, Stan, and you have developed your imaginative faculties to that of an adept without even knowing it."

For the first time that evening, Edward had told Stan something he could accept. He had an amazing imagination. That he knew with certainty.

"But why am I in danger?"

"Stan, come on, by now you must have understood more or less the plot here? Someone or some group is killing – murdering – anyone who has this gift to observe and co-create reality and, at least from what I am able to perceive, there are only a few of you left."

"But why?"

"My guess, and a guess is all it can be at this stage, is to change our reality to their advantage."

Stan's blood ran cold. He picked up and sipped his coffee, now long cold, considering what Edward had said. He still couldn't quite believe it, but his mind was racing through facts. Edward's strange introduction; the contents of his files; what he had learned on the internet and from Edward; his own ability to make things happen by imagining them; his *déjà vu* feelings when he first met Edward. He suddenly believed that he might well be in danger from some unseen enemy with some peculiar motivation to wipe Stan off the face of the planet.

"So what must I do?" he asked, more to himself than to Edward.

"We must take you somewhere safe," said Edward, "at least until we know a bit more about the situation."

"But I have a job and bills to pay and…"

"Stan, I think this will all play out very soon. Come on, let's leave. We will go to your home and get some of your things, and from there I have a place in mind. At least for a short time."

Stan nodded and reached for his coat. He suddenly felt weak at the knees and sensed a hot flush coming on. He needed to get some air at least and try to rethink through everything he had just learned so, for now, he would go along with Edward's plan. He followed Edward to the door of the coffee shop, feeling the chill in the air as Edward opened the door and waited for Stan to step outside. At that moment, time suddenly seemed to stand still and then to condense. First, he saw a small car, a black mini, moving slowly by on the road in front of him from left to right. A window was open and a masked man was pointing something out of the window in his direction. Simultaneously, he saw a small puff of brick dust to his side and a small hole appeared in the wall. He felt what seemed like a million small needles puncture his face followed by a huge pain in his left hand and then the shattering of the window to the other side of him. He watched in awe as the glass shards fell about him in slow motion. Then, just as suddenly, time seemed to speed up to normal again, as he felt Edward push him violently in the back to the ground. From there, he saw the car whizz away up the street and heard the screams of people around him as three bullets whipped by.

Chapter 9

Escape

Edward dragged Stan to his feet and started to run. Stan's face was a mass of small red dots where sharp brick dust had pierced his skin, and his hand was bleeding profusely, but Edward wanted to get him somewhere safer – and fast. It wouldn't do to go to a hospital nor have the police involved. He pulled Stan into a nearby alley and stood him up against the wall.

"Stan!" he shouted. "Stan, come on, we need to move." Stan was in shock until Edward gave him a short sharp slap on the cheek. "Stanley!"

Stan started to come around a bit so Edward began to drag him along again by his coat lapels. He had no plan since this was a quite unexpected development, but he thought perhaps to head to a bar somewhere and try to clean Stan up in the bathroom without attracting too much attention. After that, they would simply have to get a taxi and head to Edward's chosen place of safety.

"I've been shot," said Stan finally, with a look of disbelief.

"It's just a graze, Stan. Quick let's go in here." He pulled Stan into a small bar. "We'll get you cleaned up and then we will grab a taxi and get out of London."

Edward too was somewhat shocked. Of all the suspicious deaths he had investigated to date none had so far involved shootings. So why the change in their *modus operandi*? Were they now aware of his activities, and of Stan?

In the small cramped bathroom, Stan was looking at himself in the mirror. His paleness was now a sickly cream color punctuated by small red bloody spots. He had his bleeding hand under the tap. It seemed the bullet had only grazed it but it still hurt like hell. Edward grabbed some paper towels and wrapped them quickly around Stan's hand. He could already hear sirens as the police arrived at the shot-up coffee shop not a block away. They had to be fast, he thought.

"Come on, Stan. Just clamp that paper on it for now and let's go," he said with urgency.

Out in the street, Edward scanned the traffic for a free taxicab and seeing one, he hailed it and bundled Stan in. Stan didn't hear the location that Edward gave the driver as he was still dazed and in pain. Luckily, he was wearing his glasses, he thought, or else he would probably have lost an eye from that brick dust. Stan's heart was still pounding and he had a sense of unrealness about this particular reality.

After the taxi had navigated about a half a mile, Edward started to feel a bit more relaxed.

"How is that hand, Stan?" he asked.

"Hurts like the blazes," replied Stan. "What just happened?"

"They know about you, Stan. They are after you. I did tell you that you were in danger."

Stan nodded. "You did," he replied. "Where are we going?"

"Somewhere safer, Stan. Out of town to stay with a member of my Lodge. Between the two of us we can take care of your physical and psychic safety," Edward said, pulling out his mobile phone.

Stan suddenly felt very small like a child in a complicated world relying on his father or grandfather to help him navigate that complexity. Stan's life was books and all the marvelous adventures he had were through books and reading. For all of his ability to imagine, he had never actually felt so damned scared in all of his life and now he rued the day he had met Edward. Damn the feelings of *déjà vu,* and damn the thought that this reality was his. For the remainder of the journey, he sat quietly feeling sorry for himself and wondering why his comfortable little world had just exploded so dramatically. Despite the pain from his hand, despite the fear in his stomach, and despite the rising anger inside of him, he fell asleep.

He finally awoke to the sound of tires crunching over gravel. His hand still throbbed and burned. He peered out of the window to see they were arriving at quite a large country house set some distance away from the road. The cab came to a stop on the driveway and Edward paid the driver. Stan had no idea where they were, but he could see no other sign of habitation in the area except what he took to be a small gatehouse down by the driveway entrance. He stretched and then rather wished that he hadn't as it seemed every muscle ached a thousand aches. *Must be the stress*, he thought to himself grimacing. He slowly and gingerly got out of the cab and followed Edward's lead up the steps towards the front doors of the huge home they had arrived at.

The doors opened as they climbed and a woman stood there. She looked worried and concerned immediately flinging her arms around Edward. "Are you alright?" she asked him. Edward simply nodded and made his way through the door. "And you must be Stan?" she said.

For the second time in a day, Stan's world stood still for a moment as he looked into her beautiful face. Firstly, he somehow felt as if he had known this woman all of his life and maybe even before that as she looked so familiar to him, and second, he was in love. There was no doubt that despite the fact that he didn't believe in love at first sight, he was dreadfully in love with this woman. He had read about love at first sight of course, and now confronted with it; he was forced to concede that it might just exist. His heart was beating so hard she must surely hear it and his mouth seemed stuck, glued shut, so that all he could manage as an answer was a strange sort of croaking sound. *Déjà vu* struck him again, but this time he just knew that he knew and adored with all his heart the woman who stood in front of him. Yet, he didn't even know her name.

The woman he knew and had always known ushered him in

and introduced herself. "Jo," she said simply holding out a hand. Stan took the hand and shook rather over vigorously, still wordless. Jo smiled back at him. *Did she feel it too?* Stan thought rather hopefully, and then immediately discounted the idea as foolish.

"Stan," said Edward's voice from down the hallway, finally breaking the moment for Stan and allowing him to avoid Jo's gaze, at least for a while. "Come through, Stan. Jo will clean you up a bit. Jo, do you have any spare clothing for Stan? I think he needs it."

Stan looked down to discover that his clothing was indeed covered with bloodstains, dirt and orange-reddish brick dust.

As Jo went to fetch whatever clothing might work, Edward showed Stan to an ornate and lush bathroom where he could take a shower. He brought a first-aid kit from somewhere and instructed Stan to see to his cuts and bruises before re-emerging. Edward would prepare some food and, more importantly, some coffee.

After a hot shower, Stan felt significantly better. He pulled on the ill-fitting T-shirt and jeans that Edward had brought into the bathroom and looking in the mirror, even managed a chuckle as he saw himself reflected there looking like a wounded soldier. The chuckle didn't last long, though, as he now finally under-stood that Edward was right. Somebody really was trying to kill him.

Stan found Edward and Jo in a large and well-equipped kitchen. They both looked up as Stan entered having followed the sounds of their voices down the long and ornate hallway from the bathroom. "Come in," said Edward. "You must be hungry? We have some sandwiches and some coffee. Dig in and sit."

Stan did exactly as he was told, and trying not to look at Jo he started to tuck into a ham and lettuce sandwich. She filled the room for him. Her dark wavy hair sparkled in the brightness of the fluorescent kitchen lights, her oval blue eyes shone like beacons welcoming him home, and everywhere there was the wonderful scent of her. What the hell was wrong with him? he wondered.

"Jo is a trusted member of the Lodge and this is her home," Edward told him. "We should be safe here but Jo and I need to make some further arrangements. Unfortunately, whomever we are dealing with can probably establish our whereabouts using certain magical methods and there is the risk that they could try to attack us with magic too. So we should prepare some protections here."

Stan took this news seriously. He had now decided that there was something to the magical stuff. He sat munching sandwiches and looked admiringly around the well-appointed kitchen. This was a home for royalty, he thought, and far beyond anything he had ever seen in real life. He wondered how Jo could afford such a place and whether she lived here alone. He felt a strange pang of pain as he wondered where her husband might be, if she was married. Once again, Stan realized that he was behind the curve, always relying on the presence of Edward to know what to do and how to do it. He was a pawn in someone's game and he didn't yet understand its rules.

Chapter 10

Elemental Magic

The breathing was rhythmic. With each breath, she was breathing in fire. All around her were flames, and she could feel the heat and smell the acrid smell of smoke. She inhaled and imagined that the fire was entering every pore of her body like a sponge. She could feel its heat and she imagined herself expanding – expanding and flickering. She was aflame as she consumed the fire, rising and floating like hot air as she filled herself with its energies. She was burning her dross, transforming it into pure energy, cleansing herself. She then began to reverse the process, breathing out the fire through every pore in her body but feeling renewed and almost reborn as she did so. In her mind's eye, she could see the Salamanders looking at her. She would soon command them; they would do her bidding just as the Sylphs, Gnomes, and other elemental creatures would too in time. Right now, she was working to strengthen her will.

Alison began to return to normal consciousness and performed a final Kabbalistic cross, imagining the drawing of a huge cross of light in front of her while intoning a series of magical words of power. As she opened her eyes, she felt a feeling of satisfaction that her evening session was properly completed. Every day she practiced her art twice daily, once in the morning and once in the evening. After many years, it felt natural to her and if by chance she had to miss a session, she felt strange. She moved to the small desk in the hotel room and began immediately writing her realizations in her diary. This diary, and others just like it at home in Houston, contained all of her notes, realizations, visions and thoughts from her magical work and they were precious to her.

She recalled how it had all began with the discovery of a book by a magician in a second-hand bookstore in Spring, Texas. That book had changed her life and given her natural psychism and interest in the esoteric a real channel to blossom. The book had set out a series of exercises to develop magical powers focusing on the Elements; Fire, Water, Air and Earth. Along the way, she had spent many thousands of hours in meditation building her magical mirrors. This was an honest and exhaustive assessment of her faults and positive attributes which she had then assigned to each element to understand how the Elements were balanced inside of her. She had discovered that the Fire Element was somewhat dominant reflected in her high energy levels and fiery temper, amongst other things. She had moved on through the exercises to learn how to visualize, not just see things in her imagination, but also smell, hear and feel them too. She had learned how to do breathing exercises, breathing in the Elements, other qualities and much more. All of this, all the trial and error, all the ideas, images and thoughts that occurred along the way she recorded in her magical diaries.

As she had progressed through the book and its powerful exercises, things had begun to change for her. She began to see things in a different way. She recalled one morning seeing a small patch of green moss observing how bright green and truly beautiful it was. As she noticed the moss, she started to look around and observe the trees, the blue sky, the birds singing, and the amazing beauty of nature. All were symbols she had decided. Life was a moving movie of symbols that needed to be observed in order to puzzle out their meaning. That bright green moss was a little island of emerald greenness shimmering in the sunlight reflecting from the dew that had settled there. What did that mean to her? It reminded her to look, to observe, and to marvel.

Reality is a set of observed symbols to contemplate and learn from, and if we miss an important symbol, then it keeps arising in our consciousness until we finally notice, she had thought. Perhaps this explained the strange synchronicity that often occurred to people where a symbol repeatedly occurs in their lives. *It's their inner selves' way of saying – look, observe, contemplate and accept*, she had concluded. Her life had changed, she had changed, and she recalled with growing anticipation, she would soon crown all those years of hard work and practice with an initiation from a true master.

She checked her watch, and noticing that it was almost nine, went into the small bathroom to check her appearance. *Yes, that will do*, she thought, admiring how she looked in the mirror. The ringing of the room's phone suddenly heightened her rising. The moment had finally arrived.

"Hello, madam," said a voice. "There is a gentleman to meet you in the lobby."

"I will be right there," she replied.

Chapter 11

Sedgwick

The man Alison found waiting in the lobby wasn't Zeltan and her heart sank as she realized this. Once more, she was deeply disappointed.

"Alison?" asked the small balding man who was fidgeting with his phone in a chair by the door of the hotel.

"Yes," she replied.

The balding man got up and smiled a flicker of a smile. She didn't like this man whoever he was she had decided. He looked like a snake-oil salesman. "Hello, Alison, my name is Sedgwick – Adam Sedgwick," he said holding out his hand. She took it, repulsed by a damp and sweaty palm and a weak grip. *Ugh,* she thought, *not to be trusted with a handshake like that.*

"What can I do for you, Mr. Sedgwick?" she asked politely.

"Well, it's more what I can do for you, Alison, as I am afraid Zeltan is simply unable to meet with you this evening and he asked me to entertain you to dinner, pass on his sincere apologies, and to let you know that he will call you tomorrow to make alternate arrangements."

"Oh, I see," said Alison with a sinking feeling. Not only would she not meet Zeltan tonight but she would also have to put up with this horrible creature for the next several hours. *Lovely!* "Then, Mr. Sedgwick, let us go to dinner for I am starving. My stomach has not yet adjusted to the six hour time difference and I could eat a horse."

Sedgwick led her into the hotel restaurant. According to Sedgwick, it apparently had an excellent reputation for its fish dishes. He requested seating in a quiet corner. Sedgwick was, she noticed, a little on the plump side and perpetually damp-looking. He had a handkerchief in his pocket and would constantly use it to dab his face. She really did not like him.

"How do you know Zeltan? Mr. Sedgwick?" she asked with a forced smile.

"Ah, I have been a disciple of Zeltan for several years Alison. I also act as his secretary and as the secretary of the Lodge," he announced proudly. "It was in fact I who emailed you on his behalf a few months ago."

Alison shuddered inside and thought how fortunate it was that she had not known this at the time, for if she had she would never have responded. "I see, and did you arrange my trip over here as well?"

"Indeed I did. I trust you are happy with the hotel?" he said looking around as if seeing the place for the very first time.

"Yes, it's more than adequate. When will I meet Zeltan?"

"Tomorrow. Tomorrow we will have a gathering and you will be our guest of honor," he said padding his brow and showing a thin smile. "Zeltan is highly delighted that you are here as you will finalize our quorum."

The waiter hovered in the background and then took his chance to move in with the menus recommending the fish and some white wine. Alison felt some sense of satisfaction on learning this and for a moment, it put her back in a good mood.

"I look forward to that."

The fish, as it turned out, was rather good. The wine Sedgwick selected was even better but Alison learned little else regarding Zeltan, or the Lodge, as Sedgwick insisted on asking many questions about Texas. He had an interest in visiting Texas at some point in the future to find out exactly what the 'American Dream' was all about. He was, she decided, a rather insipid creature and she was quite puzzled, if not a little troubled, that this man should be a close associate of someone as powerful and knowledgeable as Zeltan. She didn't encourage him to stay after dinner and he did not seem intent on staying but rather proclaimed self-importantly, that he had a 'number of arrangements' to make for tomorrow's gathering that would best be done sooner rather than later.

She was not tired at all. It was only late afternoon for her body clock and so she took a walk around the streets exploring the city of London a bit like any tourist might.

Even though it was late, London was alive with people bustling and hustling somewhere for something. *So many sheeple,* she thought, *too busy and wrapped up in their dream worlds to understand.* She felt strangely superior amongst all these sheeple as she was about to become a member of an important magical Lodge initiated by a powerful magician. A man who had powers that these people could not possibly imagine and, if they did, would think were sleight of hand or other such trickery. These sleepers locked themselves into a dense physical existence. *They have sold their souls,* she decided before heading back to her room to meditate some more.

Chapter 12

Love and Magnetism

Stan was in his element. He had found the library. A large room lined wall-to-wall with bookcases, except for one wall where there was a fireplace containing a magnificent coal fire glowing brightly and a chair either side for reading. This was wonderful, he thought, all those books and such a magnificent environment in which to devour them. Excitedly, he was thumbing through the shelves looking for something to sink his teeth into.

"Ah there you are," said a voice and Stan's heart missed a beat as he realized it was Jo.

"Books," he said not looking at her.

"Yes, that's generally what you find in a library," she smiled.

Stan looked up and saw the smile on her lips. He could feel his knees weakening at the sight of her and the smile filled him with happiness. He wanted to laugh along with the imaginary laughter he was hearing in his head. She moved towards him and started to look through the books too. Her perfume smelled of paradise. Finally, she found what she wanted and pulled out a book with a little "tada" sound.

"This might be something you will find interesting," she said handing him the book.

"Thank you," he said.

"Come sit, we should talk."

Stan followed Jo over to the fireplace and sat down holding the book that he had still not looked at. He was so taken with Jo's attention in him that he couldn't do anything but stare rather foolishly at the vision of beauty that now sat opposite him.

"Stan, I want you to use that imagination of yours. Can you?"

"Yes," he managed to say.

"Fine, now please relax and close your eyes. Relax." Her voice had taken on a husky hypnotic quality. "Relax. You are relaxing and the more I talk the more relaxed you will become."

Stan was feeling quite relaxed and his grip on the book loosened.

"Now, Stan, imagine. Imagine that you are surrounded by the brightest bluish-white light that you can possible think of. It surrounds you, it envelopes you, it pervades every cell in your body and as you imagine this see that every cell, every molecule of your body is shining with this light and know that this light protects you and keeps you safe. Have confidence that nothing can penetrate this light." Her voice had become a drone in the background and Stan could see an electric blue-white light surrounding him as an aura. He could feel its energy; its protective energy envelop him as he sat there is his chair.

"Very good, Stan. Now, you will open your eyes when I say so and return to normal consciousness but before you do, know that this light is there protecting you even if you forget that it is. It is an impenetrable shield and it will last just as long as needed. One, two, three, open your eyes."

Stan opened his eyes still feeling relaxed and somehow refreshed to see her smiling at him from the other chair.

"I love you," he heard himself say. "I have always loved you."

Jo's smile grew as Stan blushed and looked down at his feet. How had that come out? he thought to himself.

"I know," was all Jo said, and then there was silence as the two of them sat feeling some sort of a bond or connection and listened to the crackling of the fire.

"Sometimes there is a magnetic attraction between two people, Stan," said Jo at last. "This magnetism finds its source within you. Everything and everybody has a dual aspect; an outer male and an inner female or vice versa. You can call it your soul if you wish, as it is as good a word as any, with which to describe your inner self, and for you, it is female. It has the opposite polarity to your male physical self. Perhaps you have dreamed of your soul, Stan, as a beautiful and innocent woman that you love beyond everything?"

"I have dreamt of her, yes," said Stan. "Especially when I was a boy, she was in my dreams a lot." He was thinking of the beautiful and mysterious woman of his dreams. How he felt such absolute love for this creature that so often had been part of his dream life.

"Sometimes I think that we project our soul love onto someone else. Who knows why? It could be a scent, a word, something innocent that triggers a memory and the recognition of the self-soul, and it is projected onto someone else." She continued, "When this happens we feel as if the person we have endowed with the characteristics of our own soul is the perfect being for us. The perfect match, and we feel the same love and emotions for that person as we do for our own souls."

Stan nodded because he understood. He wasn't sure why he understood but he just seemed to accept what was being said.

"In magic, this kind of magnetism can be very powerful and it can be put to good use. The book I gave you earlier is a book that deals very well with this phenomenon and a woman who knew a lot about such things wrote it. Please keep it and read it when you have the time."

Stan looked at the book. It was *The Sea Priestess*.

"I will treasure it, Jo, thank you,"

"I know that the magnetism exists between us, Stan, as I felt it too or perhaps I felt it emanating from you when we first met and I recognize it for what it is. Be comfortable with it and with me."

Stan somehow felt better but once again, he was feeling lost at sea. These things were alien to him and this unsettled him.

"Is this your house?" he heard himself say after a while.

"It is now, yes. It used to belong to my husband's family and I inherited it."

"Oh, I am very sorry,' said Stan.

"It's OK, Stan. Mark has been gone over a year now and I am

over the worst of it. He was an observer too."

Stan was stunned as he read between the lines. So somewhere, Edward had a file and the name on the front of it was Mark.

"Ah, so here you both are,' said Edward's voice from the doorway. "I had wondered where you had both got to but now I realize how foolish I am as of course Stan would be in the library," he laughed as he walked into the room. "Are we done?" he asked looking at Jo. Jo nodded her head. 'Very good," he said.

"Who is trying to kill me?" Stan asked. "And who is it you are protecting me from?"

Edward leant against the bookshelf and his face became very serious.

"There are a group of people…magicians. They are in London as far as I can tell. A very powerful magician called Zeltan leads them. I have never met him and I do not know what he looks like but he is an adept in the dark side of our art. I believe or rather suspect that it is this group that is behind these murders," said Edward.

"They killed Mark," added Jo in a quiet voice.

"Mark was my best friend and a member of our Lodge," said Edward. "He was a tremendous magician and dedicated to serving humanity."

"And so what is the plan?" asked Stan after a short pause.

"I wish I had a plan, Stan," said Edward. "The truth is I don't have a plan. We must wait and see what their next move is because we don't really know what it is they are trying to achieve or how."

"But you said they were trying to change reality," said Stan.

"I suspect they are and, in fact, logic suggests that this must be the objective but…" Edward's voice trailed off and he was obviously now deep in thought. "I must go back into town," he said finally.

"You are going to leave us?" asked Stan nervously.

"Yes, Stan, I must go through my notes again and there are some items I should like to buy too – besides, you will be entirely safe with Jo. She knows what she is doing and what we are up against."

Stan looked over at Jo who simply shrugged her shoulders, smiled and said, "Edward knows what he is doing. Do you want to borrow my car, Edward?"

Edward nodded. "I will if I may."

"I must say, you both sound extremely confident which, given what happened to me today, I find pretty strange," said Stan looking from one and then to the other.

Edward laughed briefly and ironically. "Stan, I am confident that, for the moment, you are safe but please don't get the feeling that I am not worried about the situation we are in because I am very deeply concerned. Many good people are already dead, some of whom were good friends of mine, and the only people on the planet that understand something of this situation are the three people in this room and the perpetrators."

"What are we to do then, while you are gone?" asked Stan.

"Stan, read some books and keep Jo's company. I will be back before you know it, hopefully better prepared than I am now to deal with whatever lies in front of us," said Edward. "Right, Jo, thanks for loan of the car, I will be back as soon as I can meanwhile, call if you need anything."

"Will do," said Jo. "Take care, Edward."

Chapter 13

Night Terrors

Stan had spent a few hours in the company of the lovely Jo and she had given him a tour around the house. The place amazed him with its five bedrooms, at least seven bathrooms and toilets, and was even more amazed by the large temple situated towards the back of the house on the ground floor. The temple came complete with an altar, a black and white tiled floor, two large ancient Greek-style columns either side of the altar and various large wall hangings depicting the four Elements. That anyone would have a magic temple inside of his or her home was bewildering to Stan. "This is generally where our Lodge meets," Jo told him matter-of-factly. "Edward designed it and we are rather proud of it," she said as they peered into the room.

Stan was also amazed by Jo's obvious reverence for the room which reminded him a bit of the way that Catholics behaved in their churches bobbing in front of the altar and making gestures. He could only imagine what happened in that room.

After the tour, they shared a coffee back in the library, which was evidently Jo's favorite part of the house outside of the temple room. "I too love to read, Stan," she told him. "There are over 5000 books in this library, many of which you couldn't buy for love or money."

Stan looked at the books neatly lining the robust and ornate wooden shelving and rather shamefully thought of his own books lying in disorganized piles and heaps on the floor around his small flat.

Eventually, Jo suggested that she was tired and showed Stan to one of the guest rooms complete with a four-poster bed and oil paintings lined up on the oak-paneled walls. "This is your room for the night, Stan," she told him. "I am not far away, just down the corridor."

Stan had enjoyed every minute of being with her and really had almost forgotten the earlier events of the day along with the pain radiating through the palm of his hand. Not only was she beautiful, intelligent and witty but there simply was, well, that magnetism about her. The closer he was to her, the more marvelous he felt and when she gave him a small peck on the cheek as she bade him goodnight he could feel his knees grow weak. If she noticed, she did not show it but Stan suspected that she did. As he watched her walking gracefully down the corridor he already felt lonely, but more than that he felt as if he had lost something important to his wellbeing. He sighed, a deeply resigned sigh and closed his door.

The room was almost as big as his entire flat, he thought as he lay down in the huge bed. His hand throbbed and his face felt sore too as he rubbed it gingerly. For Stan, reality had truly taken on a feeling of being unreal. In a matter of days, hours even, his cozy little world had turned upside down. He had even been the target of a shooting. Despite this, simply being a few feet away from Jo had a strangely calming effect on him. He really ought to be scared shitless, yet he felt somehow serene, and above whatever it was that was going on. He was warm, cozy and... *Wait*, he thought, *I am really quite warm*. He felt his own brow. Did he have the beginnings of a fever? He wasn't sure, but it did feel awfully hot all of a sudden in the room. He got up and checked the radiator. It was slightly warm. He opened a window and stood in the cold breeze but he was really beginning to feel uncomfortably hot. He took off the T-shirt he had been given and lay on the bed, but this didn't help at all either. He was simply beginning to boil. He stood up and tried walking around the large room – suddenly he didn't just feel hot, but terribly weak as well.

"Jo," he called rather hoarsely as he also seemed to be having trouble with his throat. It felt constricted as if someone was strangling him. He was beginning to panic a bit now as the room began slowly rotating and he had to hold on to one of the posts on the bed. Something was seriously wrong and getting worse fast.

"Jo," he tried to shout the word but all that came out was a strange rasping sound. The room was spinning wildly and Stan felt faint and near to collapse.

"Stan, think of the light," said a voice close by. "Imagine the light around you." A hand was touching his forehead and he felt himself pushed down onto the bed.

"Stan, focus, listen to me, Stan," said the voice. "FOCUS!"

Stan was trying to focus but his throat was constricting, he was dripping with sweat and the room was spinning wildly, but there, in front of him every so often, as the room went around, was a vision of beauty. It was Jo. He must be dreaming. A bad dream.

"FOCUS!" she screamed at him and then slapped him hard across the face.

He tried again. He tried to lock onto her beautiful eyes and to stop the room from spinning.

"Listen to me," she commanded him. "Listen to me. You must imagine water."

"Yes, give me water," he managed to croak.

"No, it would kill you," she said. "I said imagine water. Imagine you are like a fish surrounded by clear, cooling water. Imagine that you are breathing in the water through your gills and as you do, that the cooling water is taking the heat with it. You breathe in cool water and breathe out hot water as it takes the heat away."

Stan was struggling to make sense of this. She wanted him to be a fish and he was dying. Why?

"Stan, listen and focus. Concentrate. Breathe water. Breathe it through every pore in your body. Water surrounds you, cold, clear water. Breathe. Imagine."

He was a fish, he decided deliriously. He was a very large fish in a very large tank and through the glass, a beautiful woman was looking at him and speaking but he couldn't hear the words. He could just see the mouth moving just like a fish might in a tank. Suddenly, Stan was breathing water like a fish through his gills. It was cold, very cold. But it got hot quickly and he had to spit it out as it was burning his insides it was so hot. Surely, there wasn't enough water even in his large tank to take all of this heat. He would boil alive.

"That's it, Stan!" she screamed. "Breathe it in and be surrounded by the water."

He breathed in and exhaled. Cold, hot, cold, hot. His throat was beginning to feel better and he was definitely feeling less hot. The beautiful vision outside of the fish tank was holding his hands, he realized. Yes, he did have hands despite being a fish, he marveled.

"Keep it going, Stan. Imagine water. Breathe the water. Don't stop."

Stan was now imagining being in a river. Swimming in a mountain river and the water was foaming all around him rushing by as cold as ice from the melt waters further upstream. He was feeling more and more normal. His temperature was subsiding.

"OK, Stan, good job," said Jo.

He realized it was Jo. Somehow, she was swimming with him in the river. No, she was holding his hands so she couldn't be in a river. And then he was back lying on the four-poster bed with Jo leaning over him holding both of his hands. Her face was determined, her grip was extremely tight, and his hand was hurting like hell.

"Ouch," he screamed.

"Good. You are back," said Jo.

"What the hell happened?"

"Relax a bit and keep thinking of the light around you, Stan; an aura of blue-white light protecting you. OK?" said Jo. "Sit up if you can."

Stan hauled himself up into a sitting position. "It's OK, I feel better now."

"Unfortunately, Stan, I am not at all sure that that is the end of the matter."

"End of what matter?" asked Stan. "Surely the stress of today gave me a bit of a panic attack or something?"

Jo shook her head. "No, Stan. I think we should go to the temple for the night. We will be safer there; protected by the energy in the temple"

"Temple? Why?"

"Stan, you, or we, are under psychic attack. We must defend ourselves. That's why I am telling you to keep that light around you and imagine it; visualize it as strongly as possible."

Yet again, Stan wondered what reality he was now experiencing. "A psychic attack? How?"

"Stan, trust me. Edward thought this may happen which is why he brought you here. We will be much safer in the temple, I promise. Are you steady now? Because we should go there as soon as you are able."

He got to his feet. He was now feeling quite chilly and very damp from the sweat and he pulled the T-shirt back on before taking a few steps. "I am fine,' he said.

Jo took his hand and led him out of the room, across the hallway to the staircase and down through to the temple room at the back of the house. 'Take off your slippers please," said Jo at the door. She pulled herself upright and opened the door, bowing to the altar and making her way across to a set of chairs. "Follow me and do as I do," she told Stan. He too bowed and followed her in standing as straight and as tall as he possibly could.

"Now, let's sit facing one another," said Jo arranging the chairs. "Hold my hands and look into my eyes."

For Stan there was nothing he would like better than to do

exactly that and so he dutifully did as instructed. "What now?" he whispered.

"Let's use that magnetism shall we."

Again, for Stan, this was no problem. Her very presence sent his soul to higher places and gave him a feeling of longing. Jo smiled, "Yes, that's it. I can feel the magnetic power quite strongly and we can use this energy," she said. "Can you feel it?"

Stan could feel it. He was aching with a longing for her but there was an electrical feeling and he tingled all over from it. It was so strong he was shivering involuntarily.

"Now, Stan, feel that, take it and wrap it mentally around us like a blanket of magnetic energy," she said.

"Did you see that?" asked Stan with a worried look on his face.

"What?" asked Jo.

"The lights, they are flickering."

"Maybe they are, Stan. Stay focused on our magnetic energy and me. Pay no attention to anything else."

Stan could hear his heart beating and could taste a strange metallic taste. It was the taste of fear. The lights continued to flicker and then abruptly, they went out.

"Stay focused, Stan. We are safe in here."

From somewhere in the house Stan could hear noises. "There is someone in the house," he whispered. He could hear a pin drop as every one of his senses was working overtime straining to see, hear or feel whatever it needed to in order to react.

"No, there is no one in the house but us. Ignore any sounds, anything you see just focus on me and the energy."

Stan was trying to focus but he was sure he could hear voices and footsteps somewhere in the distance. Any second, the door to the temple room was going to burst open and they would be caught unprepared sitting holding hands staring into one another's eyes like lovers. He must do something. He must make Jo aware of the danger they were in. They would need to take cover.

"Stan!" said Jo sternly. "There is NO one here but us. Stay focused on me."

The temple door suddenly burst open clattering against the wall making Stan jump. Now they were finished and he regretted the misplaced trust he had bestowed on Jo just because, deep inside, he loved her beyond words. He expected a hail of bullets or something, but nothing happened, nothing at all.

"Stan, we are under magical attack. There is no one here but us. Stay focused please. Whatever happens, ignore it."

Time passed slowly. It does when every cell of your body is anticipating something dangerous to happen. They sat until Stan thought he could sit no more with an aching back, a throbbing hand and no circulation in his legs and yet, there she was. Looking into his eyes and holding his hands. A vision, a comfort and oh what magnetism there was.

After what seemed an eternity Jo finally spoke again. "I think it's over, Stan."

"Are you sure?" he asked with a sense of relief.

"Yes, it's over. They didn't succeed. However, they must also now know where you are so we will need to change the plan a little and go elsewhere. She removed her hands, rubbed them to restore circulation, and started to stretch. "No sleep for the wicked," she smiled.

"Just exactly how does someone attack someone else magically? I mean I could swear there was someone in the house."

"They wanted you to break the magnetism and run, Stan. Had you done so and left the temple room almost certainly they would have used the fire or some other strategy to weaken if not kill you."

Stan was both horrified and enthralled. Magic could be used to kill? A couple of days ago, he would have laughed so hard at that notion and yet right now he understood it was a real threat.

"So, Jo, what's the plan now?"

"We'll drive over to a friend's house. We should buy a few more hours there until Edward gets back," she said. "Let me quickly pack a few items and then we'll leave right away."

Fifteen minutes later, they were driving away from Jo's home and down a small country lane. It had been quite a day and night, Stan thought, adjusting the large anorak Jo had lent him to get more comfortable, and he was so tired. He just hoped that wherever they were going, he could try to get some sleep.

Chapter 14

An Initiation

Alison's day had been boring if she was honest, and not at all what she had anticipated when planning the trip with Zeltan or, as she now knew, Sedgwick. She had shuddered at that thought. "What a perfectly horrible man." After a hot shower, she had conducted her morning exercises, meditating for over 45 minutes in hopeful preparation for the day's events. A small in-room breakfast followed, as her stomach had still not caught up with the rest of her and stubbornly refused to believe that it was time to eat. After picking at the food she had toyed with the idea of taking another walk – after all, it was her first visit to Europe and this was London – but somehow she didn't really feel like it. The day was dark and gloomy and it looked cold and rather damp outside. Just the sight of the sky from her window had her shivering at the thought of going out and, just for a moment at least, she missed Houston's heat. Instead, she passed her morning re-reading the emails from Zeltan/Sedgwick on her laptop and tracing the flow of the conversation.

Their early correspondence mainly related to how and why Zeltan had found her. Zeltan had stated that he had sensed her presence and, after some investigation on the Akasha, had realized that she was at a key point in her development and needed a teacher. She had discovered that he ran a Lodge and practiced elemental magic but most of the discussion had been about her progress, issues and questions regarding various realizations she had made. It was only a few weeks ago that he had suggested the Lodge had a vacancy and he would like her to fill it. He had paid for the flights and the hotel too, knowing that she couldn't afford it.

Alison read again one response from Zeltan that had really

made her think. She had asked about balancing her everyday life at work with the life she was trying to pursue. She had written:

I am frustrated that I do not live in the moment. I am unaware and I sleep. No matter how hard I try, I am simply reacting from moment to moment to what fate throws at me. I don't appear to be in control and in those moments of foolishness when I think that I am, fate deals me an unexpected blow that I never saw coming as if to say "You Fool!"

I know that real life, the real richness, the real me and the real truth lies within me but I am constantly distracted by the foolishness of outer life. I would sometimes like to escape and simply meditate until I too see the face of God, but I have duties and obligations.

Zeltan's reply had been very useful to her. He had replied:

The magician, I think, must shut out the 'matrix' or the external world as irrelevant to a large degree. He knows it to be unreliable and almost certainly designed to sidetrack, fool and hold back oneself from the truth. Some occultists use the oft-quoted term of 'sleepers' to describe most people totally engaged with this outer so-called reality. I guess a more modern and internet-related term would be 'Sheeple'.

The magician knows that the truth can almost certainly only be discovered in the reality of the inside – in the deep moments of mediation and connection with the All or the One. He also learns that often this connection is visual, in the form of symbols that must be unraveled and understood in the same manner. The importance of the trained mind is to shut out the clutter. To be able to single-mindedly focus on that inner source of wisdom and not just during meditation, but also in our daily life. We learn to listen to our 'intuition' and we develop confidence in its accuracy or relevance in the process.

Subsequently, Alison spent a lot of her time working on training her mind using a variety of exercises. She would often sit for hours trying to keep her mind empty and thoughtless or trying to maintain a single thought. She decided to pass some time conducting the empty-mind exercise now. After about thirty minutes, she gave up. Despite all of her practice, she couldn't help anticipate what the evening might bring and how it would affect her on many levels. She was simply excited and her mind would not stay quiet no matter how hard she tried. She understood that this was definitely a flaw but she had an excuse in this instance.

A lonely lunch followed and, as at breakfast, she more or less had to force herself to eat. She spent the afternoon reading a book on alchemy, trying to decipher the strange symbols and language of the author without too much success. She was beginning to get bored and somewhat despondent. This was not at all how she had imagined the trip, and she was starting to consider that perhaps she wasn't as important and special as Zeltan had made her believe that she was. By mid-afternoon, she was feeling quiet down. *This really won't do, not much of a magician if I can't stay positive.*

Her boredom and growing frustration was finally disturbed at 3pm by a text message.

I will pick you up at 4pm. Please be ready – Sedgwick, it read.

Finally, some action! Her mood changed abruptly from depression to one of growing excitement.

By 3:50pm, Alison was at the door of the hotel with a shoulder bag carrying her robes and her magic ring. She was more than ready and when she finally caught sight of Sedgwick sitting in his car signaling to her and reaching across to unlock the door, she could almost have hugged and kissed him.

"Good afternoon," said Sedgwick. His pale pudgy face had a half smile and he looked damp. His car smelt of that dampness disguised with a cheap perfume.

"Hi," she replied settling into the seat beside him.

"How was your day?"

"Just great," she lied.

Sedgwick was rather quiet as he drove through the London traffic. He chewed the side of his mouth as he drove, she noticed. He was simply a revolting specimen of a man.

After about fifteen minutes, Sedgwick pulled up outside a Victorian house. It stood at the end of an upmarket street surrounded by a tall and ornate wrought-iron fence. Its double doors painted black and every window covered with black blinds so that, even though it was starting to get dark, not a chink of light from the inside penetrated. It was rather creepy she decided and confirmed that conclusion to herself as she noticed the gargoyles snarling down from just under the roof. Sedgwick led her to the doors and knocked hard peering sideways at her.

"Here we are," he said stating the obvious.

The door was opened by what Alison assumed to be some kind of servant, as he was dressed as she imagined a butler to dress in the early 1900s. He showed them in, took their coats and directed them to a large sitting room with lots of "Sirs," "Madams," and small bows.

"Take a seat please, Alison, and wait here. I am going to check how things look," said Sedgwick signaling to one of the chairs. "If you would like a drink please restrict yourself to water." He left dabbing his brow with his ever-present handkerchief.

Alison looked around the room but she observed nothing extraordinary, though she thought perhaps that she could smell a faint smell of incense. The room also had a well-stocked bar and she helped herself to a bottle of fizzy water and glass, as she was rather thirsty. After a few minutes, Sedgwick bustled into the room. Again, Alison was disappointed to see he was alone and it probably showed on her face as Sedgwick looked uncomfortable and perhaps embarrassed.

"Shortly, you will accompany me to the temple. Prepare

yourself," he said.

Alison nodded. This was more like it! She unzipped her bag taking out her robe and other paraphernalia and pulled them on. She then sat down and, ignoring Sedgwick altogether, closed her eyes in silent meditation. She tried to quiet her mind but once again, it was proving difficult. She felt a rising sense of excitement and there was little that she could do to suppress it.

"Are you ready?" asked Sedgwick.

"I am," she said solemnly while inside someone was screaming, *Am I ever?*

"Follow me please," he said rather dryly and formally.

He walked out of the room, Alison dutifully followed him to the right and down a long corridor to the back of the building, and then up a small spiral staircase that she guessed had once served as the servants' stairs. She noticed a number of strange paintings and drawings as they walked up. She thought perhaps that she recognized one or two. At the second floor, Sedgwick turned left and then right into a small room. It was empty save for a bench against a wall facing double doors.

"Now," said Sedgwick, "you will wait here until summoned." He turned and left Alison once again alone. Behind the double doors, she could hear voices, repetitious chanting, and she could definitely smell incense. She sat on the bench and tried to calm her breathing as she realized that she was now nervous. She had no clue as to what was going to happen to her – none.

After just a few minutes that seemed more like hours, the doors opened briefly. A figure dressed entirely in a black robe and hood emerged from the door. Alison could not see his face underneath the hood. The figure signaled for Alison to stand, and he then proceeded to blindfold her tying a black cloth around her head. He then whispered to her, "I will guide you." It was not Zeltan's voice.

With the blindfold in place, Alison immediately felt disoriented as she was guided, she guessed, through the double doors.

Almost immediately she felt something at her throat and the words "Who goes here seeking enlightenment?" She knew that the cold object pushing on her vocal cords was a sword. Without any guidance from anyone, Alison was unsure as to the correct response. "Who goes here seeking enlightenment?" repeated the voice, but louder and more aggressively.

"I do," she replied simply. "I, Alison Wentworth, seek enlightenment."

Her heart was pounding, but her voice was clear and she was proud of herself for her unwavering response. He pushed her further and further in, what seemed to Alison to be quite a distance. From the chanting that she could hear as a dull murmur, she realized that there were many more people than she had expected in this room. Finally, pushed down onto her knees, her chin was held by someone's hand and then jerked upwards. She knew that she was now looking directly at the man in front of her.

"Alison Wentworth," said the deeply mesmerizing voice of Zeltan. "You stand before us to be judged. I warn you that if we find you wanting in any way you will be executed and your soul forever condemned to the darkness. If you can prove yourself, you will join our exalted company and command the Elements as if a God."

There was silence for what seemed like forever during which Alison was sure everyone could hear her heart beating loudly. She was sweating too and she knew that already her robe was sticking to her back. She then heard Zeltan's voice again but she had no idea what he was saying. The words made no sense to her but the drone of his voice and its tone, combined with the heat and her sheer nervousness was making her feel very woozy. Suddenly, the incomprehensible chant stopped and she heard Zeltan again address her directly.

"Alison, Do you chose the darkness within the light? "

Alison had no idea. This didn't sound right to her but she was confused. No one had instructed her as to what she should say and she could now feel beads of sweat beginning to gather on her forehead. She was beginning to panic. Then, a voice whispered into her ear. It was her guide speaking.

"You say 'No, I chose the light within the darkness,'" it said. She repeated the phrase.

"Do you promise upon your very life to keep the activities of this night a secret?"

"Yes, I do," she said without waiting for her guide's help.

"Then now you must face the trial of Fire," said Zeltan in a fierce and threatening tone.

Alison wondered what to expect but then she felt an intense heat on her arm. She winced in pain as she realized that they were branding her. The pain was searing and she let out a gasp and then smelled her burned flesh. She was now feeling queasy as well as nervous.

"And the quenching of Water," said Zeltan as her hand and arm was thrust into cold water.

"The clearness of Air," she felt her arm blown on.

"The warm humidity of Earth," continued the voice as they applied some sort of goo to the wound and wrapped it gently in cloth. "Now kneel!" his voice commanded. She knelt with her head bowed. Somehow, she suddenly felt violated. She had not expected this.

As she knelt wondering what to expect next she heard Zeltan start chanting again using incomprehensible words. She found herself following the intonation of his voice as it rose and fell, rose and fell, and again she was beginning to enter a trance-like state as those words of power washed over her pulling her deeper and deeper in. Suddenly she was again shocked as the chanting came to an abrupt halt and they tore her blindfold off.

"Behold the Lord of the Elements," said Zeltan.

Alison had expected to look up into the face of her initiator; Zeltan. In fact, what she saw took her breath away. There in front of her was an altar and, above it, formed out of swirling incense and candle smoke, was a hideous face. Its eyes glowed red like fire, there was a hint of a nose, two horns and a wide gash of a mouth. As their eyes met, Alison recoiled as if hit by the pressure wave from a bomb. The horrific vision faded to darkness as she passed out, and in passing out her head was full of words as if a packet of information was unwinding and playing out in her head. She was overwhelmed with the words, the images – the entire content of the message that emanated from the smoke face, and then all was darkness.

Chapter 15

The Moors

Stan awoke as the car went over a bump in the road, or rather the dirt track that Jo was driving along. He awoke sore and with a feeling of foreboding that he put down to the dream he was having, but which he more or less instantly forgot on awaking.

"Hello again," said the beautiful Jo smiling sideways at him from the driver's seat.

"Hi," he said in a hoarse croak of a voice. "Where are we?"

Stan rubbed his eyes. They felt dry as if filled with grit and his body ached. It was dawn and small slits of sunlight were radiating through the heavy clouds creating a very strange effect. Everything looked surreal.

"Almost there," said Jo.

The car was bumping along a dirt road in the middle of a heather-covered moor and not far in front of them was a small house. A farmhouse set in the middle of nowhere.

"Where are we?" he asked again.

"Yorkshire," said Jo with a matter-of-fact tone. "North Yorkshire moors."

Jo pulled the car to a stop outside of the small house. As they opened the doors, Stan felt the damp chill and realized that neither of them was dressed to be outside in the prevailing weather. In their rush to leave, they had not brought proper coats or any warm clothing. Jo approached the solid wooden door of the house and knocked, shivering as she stood waiting. After a few moments, the door opened and a man with thinning grey hair and a ruddy complexion born of working outdoors bundled them in.

"Come on in. You must be freezing so let me put the kettle on and make you both a hot cup of tea," said the man, looking from one to the other of them and taking in their disheveled appearance and lack of warm clothing. "What the devil happened?"

Jo began to explain and the man waved them both to sit around a small kitchen table. He made himself busy filling a kettle and dropping tea bags into a well-used teapot while listening to Jo's description of the night's events. Stan thought once again how unreal it seemed that someone would be engaged in something as ordinary as making tea while listening impassively, with just the odd nod of understanding, to what he thought was a very bizarre tale. However, Stan's perception of what was real had already changed and he simply accepted that this man listened the tale without incredulity or surprise. As Jo finished, the man looked to Stan shaking his head and said, "You must think this is a nightmare?" Stan nodded. "I'm Stephen – Stephen Higgenbottom," he said holding out a well-worn and leathery hand. Stan took it and instantly winced at the pressure this man applied to the handshake. It was obvious to him that Stephen already had some knowledge of the background to the story and of whom he was.

Stan took the hot tea he offered and wrapped his hands around the mug for the warmth.

"Well, you are both welcome here until Edward gets here," said Stephen as he sat at the small table.

"We expect him later today," said Jo.

"I am thinking neither of you have had much sleep, so if you would like to rest there are things I need to do."

Jo agreed that she was tired and could use some sleep but she explained to Stephen that she was reluctant to leave Stan alone. Stephen suggested that she should rest and that he would keep Stan's company while she did so. Stan was left for a short time, alone with his tea and the view through the window. The moors were purple and the strange effect of the slits of sunlight hitting the heather emphasized the beauty of the moor. He felt an affinity for the place and a sense of safety too. The rawness and unspoiled beauty of it simply made you feel that way, he thought.

Presently Stephen returned and sat opposite Stan. "Hungry?" he asked.

Stan decided that suddenly he was very hungry and said so. A few minutes later, he was munching into bacon and eggs with heavily buttered toast while Stephen watched.

"I'm supposing that you don't really understand much about what is happening to you right now?"

Stan nodded.

"Well, I hope that you continue to maintain the defenses that Jo taught you? Believe it or not, he can kill you remotely and the very fact that he hasn't tried until now suggests to me he is toying with us."

"Who is he?' asked Stan between swallows.

"We think it is Zeltan. That's not his real name of course. We have no idea of his true identity but we do know that he is a powerful black magician who has many powerful followers. He has been ruthless in his pursuit of whatever he is trying to achieve and Edward believes that you are the last true observer. I am puzzled why you are still alive quite honestly."

Stan stopped chewing. He suddenly felt a strange coldness pass through him. It was fear.

"Why me? I mean, I am not a magician or a mystic but just an ordinary bloke who likes to read a book or two," said Stan. "I keep myself to myself and quite honestly, I don't think I have any special powers or abilities?"

"You have an imagination, Stan," said Stephen. "Edward says that an imagination like yours is an extremely rare thing." He paused for a while seeming to stare past Stan to some far off place. "Imagination is the engine room of creation, Stan. What we imagine, if it is done with intensity and clarity, has its own reality and that reality is the blueprint of this reality, do you see?"

Stan really didn't and the look on his face showed it.

"The basis of magic is the imagination. Imagination shapes things in a more plastic reality – the reality behind our reality. When it was said that faith can move mountains, it really can because reality can be changed through a willed and trained imagination. All of magic, all the tools of our art are nothing more than visual or sense aids if you will, designed to help us visualize and create in that plastic reality behind our reality. Ritual is acting out; a wand is a symbolic tool. It's all designed to focus the will and the creative imagination. For most of us, it takes a lifetime or even many lifetimes to properly develop our imaginative faculties but you, you have that ability naturally."

"How?" asked Stan now listening raptly.

"Perhaps, Stan, you were a magician in many past lives and you have developed this skill that way."

Stan wasn't sure he believed in past lives and so this was an unsatisfactory answer.

"It doesn't matter right now how or why, just that you have the natural ability to co-create reality."

"Look, Stephen, I'm sorry but I have no ability to create anything. I am nobody and I have never achieved anything in my life. I never married, never had kids, and I never really had much ambition to do anything other than afford to keep myself surrounded by books."

"That may be so, Stan. But the fact remains that Edward and this Zeltan both seem to believe that you have extraordinary skills. It's perhaps latent, but nonetheless extraordinary."

Stan was thinking. He was thinking of the one skill he knew that he had and had always had. He could make things happen. It was only ever little things but this skill, if that is what it is, had been somewhat responsible for his lonely existence. He recalled, reliving the experience in his mind, how his friends at school had thought him a freak because of the things he could do. How he had been at first asked to perform, and then had been isolated and talked about behind his back. Kids could be so cruel, he thought.

There was that one time that he and his friend had wanted to avoid the games lesson at school. He had had an idea that if it rained, really rained, they wouldn't be forced to go out in the cold and play rugby. He hated rugby. He hated all sports actually. So he had told his friend he would make it rain. He could see Tony looking at him and laughing saying "If only you could," and then imagining it raining with as much intensity as he could. He could still see the look of fear, disbelief on Tony's face as the first clouds appeared out of nowhere, and the first big fat drops of rain fell. How it had rained torrentially for hours flooding the rugby pitch and turning the sports fields into a mud-flooded mess.

After that, Tony kept his distance. A few days later, Tony and a few others had approached him and asked him to do something similar. They had egged him on and Stan had felt quite special because of it. He had decided to imagine a small fire in the wastebasket in the corner of the classroom. As they evacuated the school, he had noticed how all of his schoolmates had kept their distance talking in whispers about him. Luckily, the fire had been very small and no one had believed the fact that Stan had made it happen just by imagining it. The adults had instead blamed it on another poor boy that had a box of matches in his pocket. Stan had learned his lesson there and then and rarely used his imagination to make things happen after that. In a way, his life was ruined from that point on. He was an outcast with strange abilities and a weird reputation.

Stephen was right, he thought. He did have an uncanny ability. He could work magic. He didn't know how he could or why or how it worked, but he could. He had never thought of it as magic or as particularly unnatural. It just was. In time, he had come to use the skill passively. He lived inside his head in another world much better than this one. He lived inside his imagination and he was content to do so. He needed no one and nothing.

Stan realized he had been quiet for some time. Stephen was looking at him as if understanding that Stan was experiencing some kind of revelation. Stan said nothing. There was nothing to say. He now knew for sure that he had and had always had a skill. He had just never seen a purpose to it.

Chapter 16

A Lost Soul

Alison's heart was beating fast and loud. She dare not move nor look up. Around her, she was aware of movement and chanting. Inside her head, there was a shadow. She was not alone. She felt as if she could hear something breathing inside her head. Another existence now seemed to share her consciousness. What had she done?

She lay there prone in front of the altar for what seemed like an eternity; a shared eternity. Then, she felt hands on her shoulders, they pulled her upright, and then she was face to face with the man she knew as Zeltan. He looked her in the eyes looking from eye to eye as if checking something before finally smiling. "The seed has taken," he said. "Come, Alison, come with me." He walked her across the room and she was vaguely aware of many hooded faces peering at her with similar smiles. They sat her on a chair and told her to wait.

As Alison sat, she could hear another voice talking inside her head. The voice was indistinct as if far away and she could not quite grasp what was being said but the voice kept on talking and talking as if to itself. This would drive her mad, she thought. Then she was again looking into the eyes of Zeltan.

"Relax, don't fight the Master and all will be well. This is just a passing phase and soon you will feel more normal," he told her.

"What have I done," she murmured.

Zeltan laughed and threw back his head. "Alison, you have become as a Goddess. The world and its sleepers are at your disposal. In due course, you will learn how to use this power. In fact, I will show you. We will change everything as the Master wills it. You will see."

A cold chill ran down Alison's spine as she listened to Zeltan's words. She understood deep down inside that somehow she had betrayed herself. Her ego, her desire to be special, it had brought her to this moment and she understood it to have been a ruinous act. She had sold her soul. Tears slowly and silently ran down her cheeks. She had been fooled, but it was her that was the fool as she had wanted to believe that she was special and important. How arrogant!

"You will sleep here tonight, Alison," she heard Zeltan saying to her. "The seed will take a few hours to establish itself properly and it is best that you remain here among friends while that happens. In the morning, Sedgwick will give you further instructions. Meanwhile, I must attend to some unfinished business," he said and was gone.

They helped her up and walked her through a maze of corridors. They removed her robes and she laid her on a bed. Whoever had walked her there left, switching out the light, and Alison was alone but not alone in the room. The droning voice in her head was compelling her to sleep and sleep she did.

Chapter 17

A Stone Circle

Stan awoke. He looked around trying to recall where he was before it came flooding back. He was in Yorkshire with Jo and Stephen. Outside it was beginning to get dark and he realized he must have slept for several hours. He felt better for it. He could hear Jo and Stephen talking somewhere in the small house and he got up and followed their voices back to the kitchen.

"Hello, sleepy head," said Jo with a big smile.

"Come sit," said Stephen. "You slept well I take it?"

Stan nodded, suddenly feeling embarrassed about his appearance as he caught sight of his reflection in the kitchen window. His hair was more or less standing up on end, he still wore the T-shirt and jeans he had been given seemingly an eternity ago.

"Edward called and he is about 30 minutes away," Jo told him.

Stan felt comforted by the news. Edward knew what he was doing and more than anyone, he understood the situation – if it could actually be understood.

"Stan, I want to show you something but you'll need to put on warmer clothing, and we had better be quick or else it will be too late," said Stephen.

Jo nodded. "Yes, come along, it's worth it."

Stan reluctantly pulled on the old coat he was given and a pair of old boots. He hoped they wouldn't be going too far because he was hardly dressed for it.

Outside, it was dusk and it was cold. A chilly breeze was bending the moor grass and the whole place was damp and muddy. They made their way down a path at the back of the house with the icy breeze at their backs. The moon was occasionally visible between breaks in the clouds low in the sky, readying itself to be the main light-bearer for the night. Stan put his hands deep into his pockets to keep them warm.

"Here," said Stephen pointing in front of them.

Stan looked in the direction that Stephen indicated and saw nothing but moorland.

"I don't see anything," he said puzzled.

Then he did see. It was not obvious until you were almost on top of it because of the rocks and boulders naturally scattered on the landscape, but he saw that in front of them was a smallish circle of stones. Jo and Stephen had moved ahead of him and now stood in the center of the circle. Stan moved to join them there.

"Do you feel it?" asked Jo.

Stan couldn't say that he felt anything except bitterly cold.

"Be still and relax," said Stephen.

Stan did so. At first, he could feel nothing, but then almost imperceptibly it crept up on him. There was a sort of natural static about the place. As he tuned into the feeling the hair on the back of his neck started to stand on end, and a shiver ran through him but not from the cold.

"Yes, you do feel it don't you?" said Jo. "This is a special place of ancient magic. You see, man has known about magic for millennia. This knowledge was passed on, or obtained, through meditation and other such techniques, but always kept quiet. In a sense, it was suppressed by those who knew because of persecution or the lack of readiness of others to accept it. It was hidden. The ways of magic became arcane or occult knowledge. You know, for all of their claims and 'discoveries' scientists are not yet even as far along as some of this hidden knowledge – some of which has likely been lost. There is much more to the mental universe, and man's location at the very center of it, yet to be discovered by scientists. I know that for a certainty."

Whatever it was, Stan could feel the electricity of the place. He was the center of a wheel of energy that was slowly turning around him. For a moment, he felt as still as eternity here in the center of the circle of stones, and he understood with crystal clarity that time was simply an illusion. It was a construct of the mind designed to allow the rhythm and flow of consciousness to have meaning for, without time, there could be no movement. The center of a circle was symbolic of eternity, while the turning outside the circle was like the movement of life. An eternal return finishing at the point it had started. A journey which, without movement – and therefore the time needed for the movement – all the perceptions, the experiences, the emotions, the ups and downs, the highs and lows of life, would occur in one momentary flash; an eternal instant.

Just by being here now, feeling the electricity running through his soul, he knew with certainty that, whatever lay ahead of him now, he was up to the challenge. In a sense, whatever happened was simply an experience of the soul. Yet it could have dire consequences for all of humanity.

The distant headlights of a car slowly moving down the track to the house disturbed his reverie. Edward had returned.

By the time they had made the walk back Edward was already sat in the kitchen. He had a small glass of whiskey in front of him to 'relieve the long journey'. He also had a small bag with him. He smiled as they walked in.

"Good to see you all," he said warmly, "showing Stan the circle?"

Jo nodded.

"Right, well, we should get a night's rest and in the morning we head to London. I think our only way out of this is to turn the tables and track down Zeltan… And he is in London."

No one questioned Edward because no one else actually had a plan. Stan felt nervous but then his newly found confidence, which originated within the electric atmosphere of the stone circle, returned. Edward was right. It was time to figure this thing out finally.

"How will we find him?" asked Jo.

"Simple, he will find us," said Edward, "and, if he doesn't then we will give him some help."

Stan helped himself to a small whiskey too, but Edward snatched it from his hand as he raised it to his lips.

"Best if you don't," said Edward, "you need to continue to protect yourself for the night at least."

Chapter 18

Road Trip

As Edward turned off the motorway into London, Stan glanced backwards to check that Jo was still following them. She was. He looked at his iPhone and registered that it was around 3pm. It had been a long drive and for the most part, Edward had been silent. Stan had called his boss and reported in 'sick' and was told that perhaps he was in trouble with the law because two men in suits had been there asking for his whereabouts. Edward had laughed when Stan told him this.

"Worth a try I suppose," he said, "but rather silly of Zeltan to think you might be at work."

Stan still had no clue where they were going. Jo and Stephen, who had also joined them for the trip south, hadn't questioned either. Stan assumed they knew already.

Stan broke the silence. "Who is Zeltan?" he asked once again.

Edward looked sideways at him. "A powerful magician who seems to be backed by powerful friends," he said.

"You said you were going to consult your notes, Edward, so what did you discover?"

"Not much more unfortunately. I am puzzled as to why they shot at us, Stan. It's not been their *modus operandi* and I confirmed that."

Stan was a bit disappointed. He had expected something a bit more fundamental. Some new information.

"OK. However, I don't get it. How could I be the last observer?" he asked.

Edward was silent for a while then he sighed deeply. "Perhaps you are not the very last observer Stan, but for Zeltan you serve some purpose and it seems to me to be related to your ability to imagine so well. If I really for a moment think about it, there must be hundreds and thousands of observers and he cannot possibly have had every one of them killed. So, you are most likely correct. You are probably not the very last observer but for the purposes of Zeltan, whatever they are, you are."

Stan was dissatisfied with the answer but it seemed at least that Edward had conceded that he might not be the last observer after all.

"In fact, Stan, I happen to believe, or shall I say know, that there are spiritual beings whose only role in creation is to observe reality. Without them this," he waved one hand, "would not exist at all. These beings assure the existence of the universe, the solar system and Mother Earth but what they do not do is create any of this. They don't live life and experience like we do and so they cannot co-create our day-to-day reality. Most assuredly, it is we who do that."

Stan sat silent for a moment pondering this new piece of information.

"We are being followed," said Edward looking in the rearview mirror. "That black car behind us has been with us for at least the last two hours now. Let's try something."

Edward abruptly steered the car to the left causing other vehicles to blow their horns and at least one driver to make a rude sign as he hit his brakes. Stan saw Jo and Stephen sail by in surprise, but the black car swerved successfully and continued to follow.

"There you go. Told you so," said Edward grimly.

Edward accelerated, driving much too fast for the narrow street in which they found themselves. He immediately braked hard and turned left before accelerating again. Stan saw the black car repeat the maneuver. They were being followed. The faster Edward drove, the faster the black car followed them having lost any pretense of hanging back; it was now glued to their tail. Stan hung on to his seat as Edward made a series of sharp turns just missing one or two pedestrians. Nevertheless, it was to no avail.

The black car was stuck to them.

"I'm not a good enough driver to throw them off, Stan," said Edward, but Stan hardly heard his words because he had had an idea. He would use the very skill that had put him in this situation in the first place, his imagination. He began to imagine the black car blowing a tire. He closed his eyes and tried to shut out the screeching of the tires and the sound of his own heartbeat, which sounded like drumming inside his head as the adrenaline flowed through his veins. He saw the black car as plain as day in his mind's eye and he watched it as their front left tire exploded into fragments. He was willing it to happen so hard that he had tensed up in his seat. His muscles locked with the strain of willing, visualizing with clarity and trying to develop a sense that it was done. That it had already happened. He sat clenched with his eyes closed repeating over and over the scene in his head. Suddenly, Edward swerved hard. Stan did not see why as he was so focused on his inner imaginings. He bounced violently forward in his seat feeling the searing heat and pain of the seatbelt across his chest before bouncing back with just as much momentum but in such a way that his head hit the side window with a loud crack. He felt momentary pain as his inner vision of the black car faded to darkness.

Chapter 19

Regrets

As her eyes opened, the memories all came flooding back. She saw once again that devilish face composed of smoke, and she shivered as she understood what had happened to her. Yes, they had her initiated – into hell. She no longer heard the mumbling voice that seemed to share her consciousness and for a second, she thought perhaps that everything was fine after all. Then she felt it. It was like coldness inside; emptiness filled with a nameless malevolency. A void in her soul occupied with darkness. Silent tears ran down her face as she struggled to accept that, because of her ego, she had betrayed herself.

The room was still dark. She had no idea how long she had slept a fitful sleep filled with demons and darkness. She had to compose herself, she thought, before opening the door. She couldn't be seen to be weak. "We are strong," said a voice inside her head. It was her voice but there was a stereo effect as it combined with a much deeper and quieter voice that emanated from the indweller. She stood up and moved to the door. She tugged on the handle expecting it to resist, but it turned and the door opened. She looked each way along the corridor but there was no one there. They made a decision and turned left. She seemed to recognize the place. It had a faint but strengthening familiarity to them. As she walked, she picked up her pace and purpose, walking to the end of the corridor and down a small spiral staircase, across another hall and into a room. Before opening the door she had an image in her mind of how the room would look and she, they, knew Sedgwick would be there waiting for them.

"Good afternoon," said Sedgwick's voice as they entered. "I have been expecting you."

Alison looked at him. She wanted to scream at him. She wanted to slap his pudgy sweaty face. Instead, she found herself kissing him on the cheek and then sat down opposite him.

"You will get used to it after a while. Eventually, it will be second nature to you and when you learn how it is used, what it can do for you, you will be amazed. You have what you dreamt of, Alison. You have power. You can have anything you desire." Sedgwick's face gleamed at her as he spoke and he smiled a knowing smile.

"We all feel Him inside of us, Alison. We all learn to live with Him because He gives us what we want and asks nothing in return. The power is incredible. Incredible."

"Nothing in return?" she heard herself say.

"Nothing, Alison, because you have already given Him your part of the bargain."

"And what is that Sedgwick," she asked in a quiet voice knowing what the answer would be.

"Why you have given him you, Alison," smiled Sedgwick. "Just as we all have. It's a fair trade. You get to live a life of power, luxury, and influence – whatever you want. He has you. Us."

Alison shuddered. This was not what she had wanted, not at all. She had wanted knowledge and yes – power, but not like this, not at this cost.

Sedgwick had read her thoughts. "Oh yes, Alison. This is what you wanted. You cried out for power. We heard you. Heard you clearly through the ether and we granted you your wish. You will be grateful in the end, Alison. He wanted to give you what you wanted. He instructed Zeltan to find you and bring you here to be a part of our group. He has given you everything that you desired and more besides. He, you see, chose you. Chosen."

She knew this. She, they, seemed to know quite a lot suddenly. She was aware that the Lodge of the Elements had a fixed number of members and that just in the last few months a vacancy had occurred. She knew that He had identified her as the replacement to re-complete the group. There was little, if anything, she could have done to stop this. She was flawed and that chasm of weakness had proven to be her undoing and condemned her.

"You are now a part of an elite company, Alison. When you re-meet your Brothers and Sisters in the Lodge, you will be surprised by the company that you now keep and the friends that will support your every whim," said Sedgwick.

Alison knew who her new 'friends' were. She could see their faces in her mind as if she had always known them. As if someone else's memories shared her existence. They were politicians, actors, music icons and business people. Yes, she was certainly in select company. She felt a little of her old excitement at the thought of meeting some of these people and then caught herself suddenly feeling ashamed of that excitement. It was as if she was two people, one who regretted what she had done and yet another who was excited by the possibilities and potential of the arrangement. She realized that she was experiencing the very flaw in her personality that had got her here.

"Yes, Alison. Think about it. Savor it. Your life has changed tremendously. You are no longer a sleeper but a controller," he said emphasizing the word 'controller'.

She liked the sound of that. A controller! But another part of her was disgusted by the concept and disgusted by the presence of Sedgwick and of Him inside her head.

I can work real magic now. I have the power, she thought. *But it's wrong!* screamed the other voice. The other voice was adamant but it was growing weaker. It was fading as her resistance was fading. The part of her that desired and needed was winning. It had His support after all.

Sedgwick sat smiling as if he knew exactly what Alison was thinking. It was as if he could read her mind. Then she understood. He could read her mind as It was in both of them and It shared their thoughts as if they were one. She was repulsed and excited all at the same time. Sedgwick's smile broadened.

"Things are good, Alison, and all is as it should be. Shortly, Zeltan will return and the last piece of our puzzle will fall into place and then our power will be limitless. You will see. Limitless," he said almost drooling as he spoke.

Chapter 20

Captured

Somewhere Stan could feel a vibration. It was running up and down his leg at the same time as a sound played incessantly in his head. His head! It hurt like crazy. He groaned and felt for the origin of the vibration. It was the phone in his jeans pocket. He pulled it out and opened his eyes to look. He was sitting on a wooden floor with his back against a wall. It was dark except for the light of his phone.

"Stan? Stan, are you alright? Where are you?" said Jo's voice obviously deeply concerned.

"I have no idea," said Stan through the throbbing pain.

"We lost you. Where are you?" said the voice.

Stan pulled himself up against the wall and looked around.

"In a room," he said. "I don't know. My head…"

"Stan, are you with Edward?"

"No, just me in a dark room," he replied.

"Stan, try to help me, Stan. Try to give me something to work with. Do you see anything at all?"

Stan looked around again shining the front of his phone to peer through the darkness. He couldn't make anything out in the gloom. He tried to pull himself to his feet. His head was pounding and he realized that he had bled all over the floor as he put his hand in the cold goo that was his blood.

"Jo, I'm sorry, I see nothing. Let me take a look around and I'll call you back."

"OK, Stan, but please be careful!"

He terminated the call and gingerly pulled himself up off the floor. Using the light from the phone, he identified a small window high up on the opposite wall, but it was too high to see out of. He looked around the room, his eyes beginning to make out shapes. There were boxes. Cardboard boxes filled with something. He pulled one over towards the wall. Every exertion hurt him as the pounding of his heart echoed the pain in his head.

Standing on the box, Stan could just about see out of the window. It was obvious to him that this was some sort of cellar, as above him was a street. However, he could see very little except the pavement and the wheels of a car. He stepped off the box and worked his way around the walls of the room. Surely, there was a light? Eventually he found it and flipped the switch. Nothing, no light. He dialed Jo.

"Yes?" said the anxious voice in his ear.

"Nothing. I'm in a cellar or basement. If there is a light it doesn't work and all I can see from the window is the pavement," he told her.

"Stan. GPS," she said.

Stan understood immediately what she meant and he cut her off while searching for the maps application on his phone. He found it and opened it. There it was. What a clever girl she was to think of that. There was his location on the map. He called her back.

"Somewhere on Grosvenor Lane," he said excitedly.

"OK, we are on our way. Any other clues as to where on Grosvenor Lane?"

"None I'm afraid but I do think that the black car that chased us is parked outside," he said suddenly, putting two and two together and hoping he hadn't made five.

"OK. Be careful, Stan,' she said.

Stan sat down again. Despite his head, he felt somewhat pleased with himself.

Chapter 21

Zeltan Speaks

Stan had sat for several minutes holding his phone just in case Jo called back when he heard footsteps. He thrust the phone back in his pocket and sat still his heart beating hard. The door unlocked and then opened.

"Edward," said Stan. "Thank God. I had feared the worse."

Edward stood back and two other men entered the room picking Stan up roughly and bundling him forward towards the door.

"Edward? What's going on?" said Stan as confusion replaced his initial feelings of relief.

"Stan, so pleased to make your acquaintance finally," said Edward.

"What?" was all Stan could say, now deeply confused.

They pushed him in the back again. In the general direction of the door and he stumbled towards it almost falling into Edward in the process.

"Be careful with him please," said Edward sternly.

"Edward, what the hell is going on?" said Stan. Stan looked to Edward as he asked the question. Was it Edward? he thought. It looked like Edward but this Edward was not wearing the suit and tie he normally wore but some kind of robe. "Edward?"

"Edward?" said Edward. "Edward isn't here."

"But Edward…" Stan started.

"Edward isn't here," Edward repeated. "My name, for the record, is Zeltan."

Incredulity replaced Stan's initial shock. "But you are Edward," he said half as a statement and half as a question.

Edward laughed. It was a deeply shocking type of laughter. It was both guttural and deep. Not at all like Edward's laugh. In fact, he had never really heard Edward laugh. He was pushed again in the back falling onto the stairs in front of him.

"Get up,' said one of the two men. "Up the stairs."

Stan picked himself up and started to climb the stairs. His mind was racing. How could this be? Was this Edward's twin? If it was then why had Edward never mentioned that his twin was Zeltan? He had a strange feeling in the pit of his stomach as he thought this, because all of a sudden things were slipping into place in his mind. He let out a sob, as he finally understood that Edward and Zeltan were one and the same person.

"You are Edward," he heard himself shout. "You are."

Another push in the back and he had reached the top of the stairs. The light hurt his eyes and now he could see the thick sticky blood on his T-shirt and hands. Another shove in the back propelled him across the hall and into a brightly lit room. Zeltan and the two men followed.

"Sit," commanded Zeltan.

Stan sat on the nearest chair. It was Edward but it wasn't, he thought. The sweptback hair and the face were Edward but the eyes belonged to someone else, Stan decided.

"Let me tell you a story, Stan," said Zeltan sitting down opposite him. "It's a good story. I think you will like it because you like stories."

Stan pushed his glasses up his nose and nodded meekly.

"Once upon a time, Stan, there was a magician who wanted to work real magic. He worked hard at his art. He endlessly meditated evoked, invoked, and performed rituals. He did all of the usual bullshit. But you know nothing much happened. Oh yes, he learned a good deal about himself and decided that learning about the self was a waste of time. Who cares?" Zeltan laughed again. "Twenty-five years of hard work, Stan, and what was his achievement? Squat, zilch, fuck all. He knew all about the Tarot, he knew all about spirits, memorized the kabbalah, spent months, if not years, with the Emerald Tablet and for what?"

Stan opened his mouth. He wasn't sure what he was going to say but he was interrupted anyway.

"Magic? Is it really just Jungian self-analysis? I mean, is it really just a bunch of incense and frolicking around in strange outfits mouthing even stranger words? What's the fucking point? They say that magic is the ability to change consciousness at will. After all the time he had dedicated to magic, he wasn't interested in changing his bloody consciousness! He wanted those changes in consciousness to actually change his reality. He wanted to do real magic. Physical magic, you know? Make things happen."

Stan nodded more out of pure fear than understanding.

"And then he read somewhere that scientists thought that we live in a matrix, like the fucking movie you know? What the hell could they know? Magicians and mystics have always been the only ones privileged to unlock the secrets of reality. We were the guardians of the knowledge. That's why it's called occult, because it's hidden, jealously, and possessively guarded by the few from the masses. Throughout history, it has been that way and for good reason. This kind of knowledge can't be shared with those swine. Who the hell do they think they are with their idle dreaming and super-collider experiments to start revealing such secrets? Have they spent their entire lives learning about themselves, learning how to control their thoughts, how to invoke elementals? Hell no. They have no fucking idea what they're doing, what it means for us, and reality itself."

Stan sat rapt. Zeltan's face oscillated strangely between that of Edward and something much more sinister as he spat out his monologue.

"Do you see, Stan? These scientists with their double-slit experiments and theories about bloody cats in boxes, they are unraveling thousands of years of our occult knowledge and giving it away to a world full of idiots. The sleepers are being handed reality on a plate. They are being spoon-fed our secrets by a bunch of so-called educated people who don't believe in anything except hard materialistic science. It won't do at all."

Zeltan wiped spittle from his chin and continued.

"So, there was this magician. This very seriously accomplished magician, who had dedicated his life to knowing himself and learning as much as possible about reality though the various occult systems. He realized that it had been all been for nothing because of science. How do you think Edward felt, Stan?" he shouted.

Stan nodded miserably. A mad man, he thought, and one responsible for multiple deaths confronted him.

"Yes, Stan. People had to die. People who should know better that started to mix up this scientific nonsense with proper magic. Those people who gave away our secrets too easily and educated the sleepers through their books and websites. They had to die. HE said so. These people broke the vow of silence that all magicians have made through remembered and unrecalled time and the penalty for that Stan has always been death."

"HE?" Stan whispered.

"Yes. You see, Edward stumbled on a book one day, a very special book. The only book ever written that truly set out the way to proper magic. Believe me, all the other books are just airy fairy nonsense. They comprise garbled hints and pointers hidden in pictures and words but they are actually of no real value to the genuine magician. This book, however, it showed the way clearly and purposefully. It was obvious to Edward as soon as he read it, that this was the real thing, the real path to power. After twenty-five years of practice and effort, there was no need for Edward to follow the book in its entirety because it might have taken another twenty-five years or more, to follow the system it outlined. So he took just the bits that seemed relevant, the juicy stuff and practiced that. A real spirit contact rewarded his efforts. A spirit so powerful but so in need of a vehicle, that Edward knew it was the only way to become who he really wanted to be.

He became me because of Him."

Stan watched in horrified fascination as Edward's face shifted back and forth between the Edward he knew and the demonic entity that now possessed him entirely.

"He showed Edward how to master proper magic. How to change reality and, in return, he promised to help Edward stop the scientists' betrayal of our secrets. Just as I, Zeltan, have brought people to me by showing them how to get what they want in return for their help in keeping the sacred science out of the hands of the materialists."

Zeltan had a look of triumph on his face. Stan shivered as he mentally pieced it altogether. But what exactly did Zeltan need of him?

"Yes, I am glad you ask,' said Zeltan reading his thoughts again. "All the pieces are now in place to complete the work, My Texan princess and Stan the great imaginer himself! Tonight, Stan, we will take everything back to the way it was. The few will know and the masses will serve. Science will become sacred once again."

Zeltan stood as if to leave.

"Prepare yourself, Stan. Tonight we will put that imagination to some use," he said and walked out leaving the two burly men to guard him.

Stan was shocked. It somehow made sense but nonetheless, it was shocking. He had grown to like Edward. He couldn't stop thinking about how Jo would feel. How Edward had had her husband killed! Then he remembered the phone in his pocket and that Jo and Stephen were already on their way. The two burly men were watching him so he would have no chance to use the phone.

"Do you have a bathroom?" he asked looking from one to the other of the men.

One of the two agreed to escort him to the bathroom that was just across the hallway. Stan closed the door behind him and locked it. He switched on the tap and took out his phone. He could text a short message but what would it say? *Edward is Zeltan. Be careful. Zeltan IS Edward!* He wrote finally. He sent the message and then flushed the toilet and washed his hands under the running tap before unlocking the door. The man stood there looking at him suspiciously and then walked him back to his seat across the hall. It was lucky that he still had his phone, he thought, as he sat heavily on the wooden chair to wait and to think.

Chapter 22

Rooftop Magic

"How are you feeling, Alison?" asked Zeltan as he entered the room. Alison wasn't sure how she felt. There was some kind of struggle still going on in her head and it began to make her feel irritable and tired.

"Ah, not quite done yet," said Zeltan without waiting for a reply. "Sedgwick, I think now is the time."

Sedgwick nodded vigorously. Little beads of sweat had again broken out around his forehead and he carefully dabbed himself with a handkerchief.

"Come on, Alison. Pull yourself together and follow us. This is the moment we have all been waiting for."

Alison was puzzled. Surely, she had had her moment already? However, she followed them anyway. She didn't feel as if she actually had any choice in the matter. They went up several flights of stairs before finally moving out onto the roof of the building. The roof at the back of the house had been modified to form a balcony of sorts, and on the balcony, she noticed a cleverly disguised altar. Here, outdoor rituals could be conducted in relative secrecy as there were no neighbors overlooking it and, unless you were in a helicopter, no way to observe this part of the roof.

"What do you think, Alison?" asked Zeltan waving his hand around the magical space created on the roof. "Sedgwick fetch the others please," he barked.

It was quite dark and most certainly cold out there on the roof, but the lights of the city dampened the blackness so it was quite possible to see without additional lighting. The floor comprised of alternating black and white tiles, and four small ornate candle-holders were positioned at each of the quarters.

"Nice," she said.

"Not just nice, Alison. I had this specially built. It has the correct orientation; it's protected from the wind so that the air is calm and still. It's perfection. The size, the dimensions, and the angles all carefully plotted to a certain alignment. And, on a night like tonight, with a full moon behind London's clouds, meant to be used for a singular purpose," Zeltan said.

As he spoke, his eyes seemed to be on fire and he had a certain look about him. His face appeared to distort periodically. At first, she thought perhaps that she imagined it. After all, he was rather animated. Then, Alison realized that his face really was changing between his face and that evil face she had seen the previous evening hanging menacingly over the altar. She shivered recalling the shock of the moment, and the horror that had passed through her body and soul as she looked into the eyes of the thing that now had a place inside her too.

"Alison, I chose you for this moment. He chose you. We will change the very nature of reality here tonight, Alison."

Alison thought that Zeltan sounded something akin to a Texan firebrand hell 'n' damnation preacher man. He appeared to be completely possessed. Not just by whatever spirit it was that occupied some part of them both, but possessed by sheer ambition. She wasn't sure what he had in mind, but she knew that she didn't want to play any part in it. "We must. It's our destiny!" screamed that ghastly voice inside her.

"We must, it's our destiny," she heard herself say in a small voice.

Behind her, she heard footsteps coming up the stairs. Sedgwick was back, she thought. Actually, the man appeared wasn't Sedgwick at all. He was dressed in jeans and a T-shirt and his head was bloody. He looked dazed as he reached the top of the stairs stopping to push his glasses back on his nose and looking all around him.

"Ah, Stan! Good to see you again and so glad you could join

our little party tonight," said Zeltan. "But we still miss one of our players? Sedgwick, is there no sign yet? I should have thought she would be here by now."

Stan looked past Alison directly at Zeltan. Alison could see hate in Stan's eyes. But those eyes; they were deep. They drew you in like pools of azure blue water. Even through the lenses of his glasses, Alison marveled at the depth and intensity of them. Who was he?

Sedgwick had gone again, leaving the three of them on the roof. It seemed to Alison that at least two of them had no desire to be there but the voice in her head kept muttering incessantly. It told her that she would play an important role in shaping the destiny of the entire world. That she would be revered as a Goddess after this night. She liked hearing that. It sat well with her.

"Stan, come to me. Come here," said Zeltan.

Stan slowly walked over like a condemned man, with his head hanging on his chest and a look of resignation on his face. His eyes were crystal pools of melancholy.

"Good. Sit here. Cross-legged is fine. Alison, you too on this side please," said Zeltan pointing to a spot on the roof that Alison moved to. "Very good. Now we await just one more actor in our little drama. She should be here very soon."

Alison sat wondering what on earth was about to happen. They wore no robes. There were no candles, no incense. Nothing, in fact, that would suggest a ritual. Nor were there any of the other members of the Lodge. Just this man, Stan, who she understood to be here against his will. But then, in a way, wasn't she also here against her will? The voice inside her head chided her for that thought and reminded her of the fact that this moment was why she had been born. She smiled at that. Despite everything, there was a sense of rising excitement inside her. But her thoughts were shattered by more shouting and commotion below them in the stair well.

Sedgwick was back again. This time accompanied by a struggling and hysterical woman. Behind them two burly men were dragging another older man up the stairs also. He was also struggling but well overpowered by the two giants who forced his compliance.

"Stan!" sobbed the woman.

Stan looked up also disturbed from whatever thoughts he was having. His face showed great concern and pain as he shouted back "Jo!"

The man and the woman were shoved towards Zeltan who appeared to draw himself up to full height. He looked menacing. Tall, gaunt and with a half-human face that pulsated between that of Zeltan and the other nonhuman face.

"Sedgwick, really! We have no use for him. Throw him off the building where he can do no harm," said Zeltan with his eyes focused on the woman called Jo.

Alison watched dispassionately as Sedgwick and his two burly helpers threw the man off the roof. He hardly resisted nor did he make a sound. He simply looked speechless as he disappeared over the edge of the roof. The woman he was with fell to her knees crying silently as Stan tried to reach out for her hand.

"My sweet Jo, it's so good of you to answer Stan's text with your delicious presence. You are needed here tonight, my beauty," said Zeltan.

Stan and Jo held hands. It was somewhat touching Alison thought but weak. Tears streamed down Jo's face but Alison suspected they were tears of anger. So much anger. Jo spat at Zeltan as if to confirm Alison's suspicions.

"You bastard, Edward," she screamed. "You utter bastard."

"Oh come now, my sweet. That's not very nice is it?" replied Zeltan with a smile. "Besides, who is this Edward? There is no Edward here. He is dead."

"You may leave us now, Sedgwick, and take your boys with you please. All will be well. And now the time has arrived for us to work."

Sedgwick nodded and the three of them left. Sedgwick was smiling as he wiped his brow taking a last look at the four of them on the roof. He had an air of expectation about him.

Chapter 23

A New Reality

Stan held Jo tightly as she sobbed into his chest. His mind was empty. Stephen had been thrown off the roof like a sack of worthless garbage and Stan was simply in a state of shock. He felt powerless. Betrayed, fooled, and lost in some madman's alternative take on reality.

"Well, children. Here we all are at last," smiled Zeltan standing over them. His shadow writhed in the moonlight as if it were comprised of hundreds of tightly wound snakes. Stan was horrified.

"This requires no ritual, no tools, no magic circle, or any other such nonsense," he said. "No, but still, this is the ultimate act of magic and each of us has a unique role to play in this magnificent moment."

Zeltan paused. Whether for effect or simply to savor his moment of triumph, Stan couldn't tell.

"As I explained to Stan a little earlier, we live in a liberal but materialistic era; one in which materialism is on the brink of unlocking the secrets behind magic, and science is usurping both the secrecy, and indeed, the selectivity of the knowledge. On the one hand, science is knocking on the door of understanding the keys to the very fabric of reality and, on the other, these blind fools know not what it all means and how it is used. Imagine how fast news will travel over the internet and TV when the secret is unveiled in the ignorance of their materialistic prattlings. Imagine how the sleepers will awaken and how they will soon progress. They will achieve in a short time what it has taken some of us millennia to achieve. This must not be allowed to happen! The sleepers are not ready. They are unprepared to wield such power. It must be jealously guarded as a secret as it has always been for the few who are truly prepared." Zeltan paused and cast his eyes, those pulsating eyes, slowly over his captive audience. "Furthermore, The Lord of the Elements will not allow his substances to be tampered with any further. The creatures of the Elements are hidden and they will remain hidden except from those chosen to know them and enjoy a relationship with them."

Stan was listening but not truly comprehending. Jo still sobbed into his chest and the other woman looked as if she were experiencing some form of sexual rapture. It was a bizarre scene and Stan was having difficulties processing it, and yet, there was that feeling again. *Déjà vu*. Somehow, this entire speech, the situation, seemed vaguely familiar to him. Why was that? Had he dreamed this?

"Alison, you are here because, like me, you hold the Master inside you. Like me, you desire the secret power and you are willing to give everything and anything to achieve it. Oh yes, Alison, you are a deeply flawed woman but one with a focused ability to achieve and now, you have achieved what you always sought. Alison, you are the female to my male. You are the moon to my sun. We are a pair you and I. You are my divine priestess. You complement me. The resulting magnetism between us is the magical power of opposites, of polarity."

Zeltan turned his attention to Stan leaving a visibly pleased Alison smiling broadly.

"Stan, you are the natural magician; the Fool. Your meandering imaginings through your love of books has honed your visualization skills to the level of that of the very greatest magician. Your idiotic life in books and enjoyment of the unreal has led you here, and tonight, with our help, you will un-imagine science. You will destroy science. You will change the actuality of the quantum world with the help of the Lord of the Elements."

Zeltan focused his attention on Jo.

"Darling Jo, your role is similar to Alison's. Stan chose you the moment he met you to be the moon to his sun, his priestess. Your polar presence will help build up the power that will propel his un-imagining, focused through the lens of power that the Lord of the Elements provides in the form of Alison and I, into the very fabric of actuality. In changing actuality, reality will also permanently change. Science will collapse. Overnight, scientists will be discredited. They will be laughed at and ridiculed for their stupidity and all will be well again."

Zeltan had now laid out his plan. From Stan's point of view, he wished that it were the babblings of a crazy man but Stan already knew that it was possible.

"You can't force me, Zeltan," said Stan defiantly. "I have free will."

Zeltan laughed. He threw back his head and laughed deeply. That laughter seemed to shake the very foundations of the building. Already, the magic power was building. The combination of the four of them, with the fifth in the form of the spirit that now possessed Zeltan and Alison, was somehow the key to the magical power that was building. Stan could feel it as the laughter pervaded everything, shaking the particles around him and those that composed his body. Stan understood that somehow, each of them symbolized one of the Elements: Fire, Water, Air and Earth and the 'Lord of the Elements', whether spirit or unholy demon, represented a diabolical quintessence.

"Stanley, Stanley, Stanley, my dear boy. This moment has already happened. There is no free will involved in this at all. You see, time isn't linear, Stan. You are not moving from the past to the present through a now. No! Time is a construct of the human mind simply designed to provide some order and framework for you to perceive and experience actuality as reality. You have already changed this actuality and reality in the eternal instant that IS, Stan, and now we simply wait for the moment point to arrive at that in our conscious reality at which we will register it, process, and experience it. That's the whole point, Stan. There is no act to perform, no choice to make. It's already done but, for now, the actual act seems still in our future, which is soon to be our present and then our past. Then the whole world will become aware of that new actuality as it reflects itself in the fabric of that reality that everyone experiences. You see, Stan, you are not just the last observer. You are the ONLY observer. Each of us represents the qualities of the four Elements and each of us is bringing an elemental energy to bear now that will shortly collapse itself into matter and form a new reality. Quantum physics will no longer exist because all of its rules, the very framework of existence, will have changed."

Stan knew that Zeltan was telling the truth. He knew it just as surely as he now remembered this moment somewhere deep inside his consciousness. He still could feel the power building. They all could. He could hear, feel and see a throbbing and pulsating as everything was gradually beginning to vibrate. The entire universe was beginning to oscillate. He knew that it was just a matter of time before their consciousnesses met that event in human created time. There really was absolutely nothing that they could do – nothing. It had already happened in the future, in that eternal instant, and soon, it would become the present, and then the past, and that would be it. The vibrations were growing. It seemed as if the entire universe was beginning a new dance.

Zeltan stood looking up in some sort of rapture. Both he and Alison were slowly raising their arms to the sky in unison. Their faces were pulsating, their bodies were vibrating, and soon they would experience the moment. Was this his doing? If so why? Stan felt somehow crushed. He was responsible.

Then he had a thought. It streaked though his head like a missile and exploded there unraveling as a packet of information inside his head. Zeltan abruptly looked at him. His eyes showed that he knew.

"Stan – NO!" screamed Zeltan.

Stan felt the weight lift from his shoulders, as he understood something. He had read it. There were an infinite number of possible realities according to quantum physics. Why did their consciousnesses have to continue to exist in this one?

To Stan, it was as if the entire universe had pulsated to an ultimate frequency, and for an instant, he knew that it had changed. An explosion of energy had transformed everything and collapsed itself into new types of particles. It was occurring in this eternal present moment. Reality was now just as Zeltan wanted it to be. In a way, he had won, but he had also lost. Stan had imagined. He had visualized the four of them flipping from that reality to another. They had migrated to that other reality in which everything remained unchanged. In this reality, nothing at all had happened. Everything was just the same as it had always been. He opened his eyes. Yes, nothing at all had changed. There had been no explosion, no energy, no new types of particles. Science still existed and so did he.

"What have you done? NO, Stan, you have destroyed me," screamed Zeltan, slowly sinking to his knees, his face fluctuating more and more rapidly between his own and that of something else. Jo finally stirred from Stan's chest and turned to watch, as Zeltan seemed to become just a ghost of atoms and particles hanging in space. He returned to a normal solid physical person for an instant before abruptly collapsing, dead, on the floor of his open-air sacred space.

"Poor Edward," said Jo. Stan nodded as he looked at the face of Edward. It was Edward, he thought, not Zeltan. But both were now dead.

Alison still stood. She was in some kind of daze and then she sat abruptly with her head in her hands. She sobbed silently.

Stan took Jo's hand.

"It's time to leave this place," he said as he helped Jo up. They walked arm in arm supporting each other to the stair well. No one stopped them leaving. It was as if a presence had gone taking with it whatever powers it had once granted to the Lodge members. That presence was now in another reality where, most likely, it reigned supreme.

Chapter 24

Polarity

Stan lay enjoying the warmth of the sun on his body and the warmth of Jo's body pressed next to his. With his eyes closed, he was imagining that they lay within a wheel, at its very center. The wheel turned but the center was static. Here, he enjoyed that eternal moment outside of time.

"Come on you two love birds," shouted Stephen's voice in the distance. "Come and have a cup of tea."

Stan sighed. He could just as well imagine a better cup of tea than Stephen could make in his old cracked pot. He and Jo ambled across the moors arm in arm, slowly and reluctantly leaving the stone circle behind them. Stephen was recovering. He still had to use a stick to steady himself but, for his age, he was doing remarkably well for someone thrown off a four-story building.

Jo smiled into Stan's face and he couldn't resist a stolen kiss. How happy he was. How vibrant his life had become because of that magic between them. That strong and pure magnetism. As Zeltan had said, they were like the sun and the moon; priest and priestess. Yin and yang. They were happy together.

Edward would have been delighted.

Chapter 25

Eternal Returns

Alison was driving fast. Her little sports car was screaming along I-45 towards Dallas, music blasting loudly from the car's speakers. She was on her way to a weekend retreat with some like-minded people there and she was going to have some fun. There was quite a pagan community in Dallas she had discovered, and she had quietly become a part of it on her return to Texas.

It had taken several months to recover from the traumatic experience of London. Sometimes, she still thought she could hear a small voice inside of her head, but she convinced herself it was just her mind playing tricks. Her psychoanalyst agreed and told her that it was most likely simply down to stress. Alison was pleased with her progress.

Of course, she was still just as interested in magic, but she had become much more relaxed about it and spent more time enjoying herself with friends. She had made quite a lot of new friends and found that she delighted in dancing and music. Her new approach to life seemed to be paying dividends.

There was a little ripple of excitement building inside her because just the previous week, in a small bookshop in Dallas, she had found a book. The book intrigued her. It was the only book she had ever read that seemed to show a way to train to do real magic. Of course, she had had to buy it. She had soon decided that she wouldn't take too serious an attitude to the exercises in it though because she already knew enough to cherry pick just the best bits. She would see where it led.

Acknowledgements

I conceived this story in a pub in London about 6 years ago during a discussion with my eldest son Paul about magic and the nature of reality. He kept telling me to write it so, Paul, here it is! Many thanks also go to SC Vincent who read this during the writing process, and encouraged me to keep writing until finally done. The writings of Anthony Peake, Dion Fortune, Franz Bardon, and many, many others, inspired this story. Thanks also to Liam F. Vasey and Jon M. Vasey for their encouragement and comments on the story. Also thanks to Paul for his editing. Finally, thanks to Gabriela for putting up with a few weeks of very obsessive behavior as the story developed…

About Dr. G. Michael Vasey

Dr. Gary (G.) Michael Vasey writes extensively across a number of disparate areas in which he has a passionate interest.

He is the author of over 200 articles and several books in the energy & commodities industry, two books of poetry, and several books about magic and our ability to shape our reality. He now lives in Prague in the Czech Republic, but is British by birth.

He also blogs at Asteroths Domain (http://www.asteroths domain.com) and The Mystical Hexagram (http://www.mystical-hexagram.com) on the nature of reality, esoteric sciences and magic, and about his adopted homeland at Discover The Czech Republic (http://www.discoverczechrepublic.com).

His website (http://www.garymvasey.com) showcases his entire portfolio of writings across energy and commodities, poetry, the occult and esoteric, as well as articles about the Czech Republic.

He is the author of two books on aspects of the occult including *Inner Journeys: Explorations of the Soul* and *The Mystical Hexagram: The Seven Inner Stars of Power,* two books of poetry, and several books on the energy and commodities industry.

Roundfire Books, put simply, publish great stories. Whether it's literary or popular, a gentle tale or a pulsating thriller, the connecting theme in all Roundfire fiction titles is that once you pick them up you won't want to put them down.